BIOLARITY

STEPHANIE MALONE

WE WATCH FROM ABOVE

AND PLANT THE SEED

TO CREATE THE SPACE

FOR LOVE AND HATE

THEN WAIT FOR IT

TO DISSIPATE INTO . . .

INOGENUE.

-Casualties of Science-

The setting is the future.
It is a time of death.
All is a wasteland.

The sun has expanded. The angry star spits her fire on the rock of humanity; leaving the surface of Earth, once lush with green life, charred and empty. The soil has become barren and ugly. All of the souls on the planet have been spent and as a result, there are no molecules left to create plants or human life. Seeds will not germinate to produce a new energy source. Eggs will not fertilize and bring in the next generation.

The world is broken, unable to procreate. The terrain crawls with people void of humanity; robots, exploiting science and the innocent. They go on living forever, reproducing the machine until there are no mortals to conceive.

The new culture ignores this decimation because no one can imagine a solution. Once the youngest of this civilization pass to the afterlife, there will be no more human creations, no more plant life, and no more bacteria. Our globe will be vacant like the moon. Alone. The dust and decay of what a world once was.

bi · o · lar · i · t y
1.   the bonding of plant and human DNA.
2.   an alternative to Nanotechnology.

nan · o · tech · nol · o · gy
1.   the level of technology that deals with dimensions of less than 100 nanometers, dealing mainly with the manipulation of individual atoms and molecules and the parts that make them complete.

sin · gu · lar · i · ty
1.   the result of being singular/single.
2.   the exact point in which a singular entity or idea takes an infinite value, like that of a black hole.
3.   a time in history when the computer intelligence surpasses the intelligence of the human mind and capabilities.

Biolarity is the answer for those who can afford an organic upgrade. This new science promises a shield from the sun's liquid cancer on Earth, providing refuge. Those who have chosen to remain true to the land, untouched by the devil's machine, hide in compounds underground, sheltered from the swollen luminary orb. Dirty and malnourished, these people struggle for their life, counting the days until a return to the surface is possible.

Nanotechnology is a science and study of small things to the extreme. Computer technology is combined with the microscopic size of a nano-chip. This concept is spread across all science fields, such as biology, chemistry, and engineering of body systems.

When brought together, nanotechnology seems to be the savior to the natural breakdown of the human form. Those who have nanotechnology do not worry for they will live on. Youthful forever, thanks to the continuous rejuvenation of atomic structures by their mechanical counterparts. This is only an imagined salvation because no computer could ever replace the human cellular makeup. The offspring of the nano, a new race, is torn between appearing to be human and the beating heart of a machine, fighting to be real.

Singularity is a realized beast encroaching on our human existence. The biological intelligence of the human creation is surpassed by the capabilities of the computer. With each upgrade to technology, the size of the machine is reduced until finally, a microscopic computer chip is created and joined with the body. The goal is to create a superhuman, however, the result is catastrophic to the survival of the mortal race.

As all things on earth must whither and die, so must the mechanical constitution of the mainframe chip. Through use and exposure to bodily fluids, the chip begins the cycle of decomposition. What was once praised as an antidote to the human condition is now cursed as the devil in disguise.

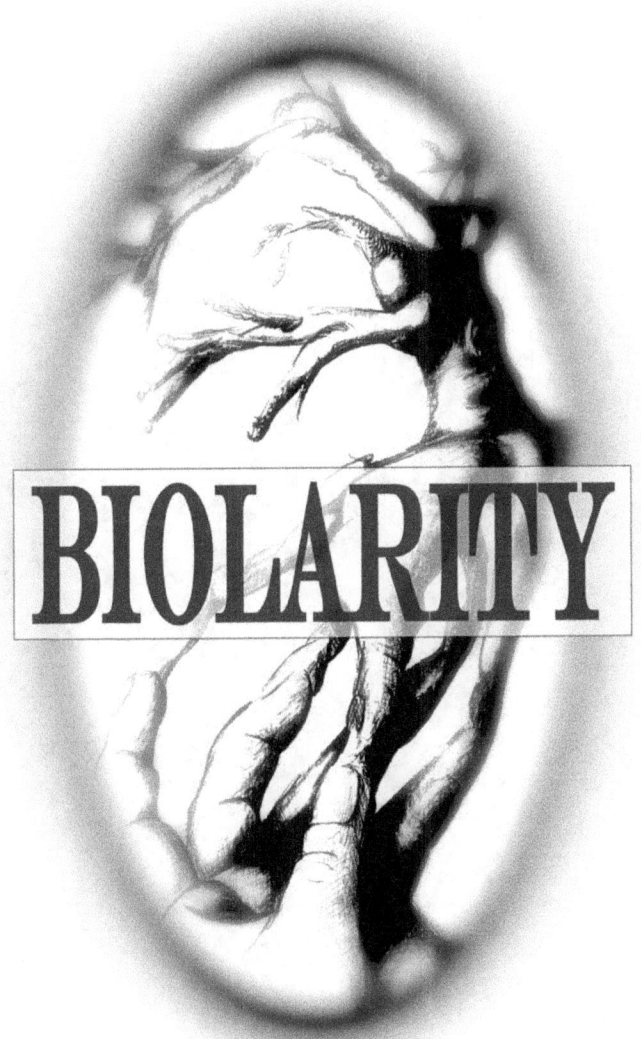

BIOLARITY

-THE INOGENUE-

There lived a Gen some time ago, who knew the gifts were great, and was presented with the choice of free will to use them as good or as evil... all is at stake.

It is the time before time, when the Earth is just a spark, trapped in the wandering tide of the universe. The Inogenue travel the rippling currents of black matter and stardust to find the perfect starseed, the one that will grow to be their home. There are only two currents of emotion in which an individual can manifest: the side of illumination and the opposite side of darkness.

One can choose the path of bitter hate, drawing more darkness into the soul's empty voids until there is no light left. Then there is the equal and opposite feeling of love, joy, and happiness. When a being feels love and shares affection, the feeling grows and spills onto others. The illumination is strong and there is love in all the space between. Depending on the collective consciousness of the whole, a nation will become enlightened and prosper, or broken and devastated.

The Inogenue know this unyielding lesson the most. They watch as their home planet is overrun with hate and greed. They watch as the innocent are ruined. A few are able to leave the destruction and begin their lives anew.

Essuel and Annuil are only small boys when their father escapes with them. He hides with his family on the uninhabited space of Venus. He creates a palace for them and begins his development of the new planet from the chosen neighboring starseed. Their new home, Planet Earth, will be guided with love.

The brothers grow in age and in jealousy, tainting the father's plan. Although Essuel is the eldest brother, Annuil will take the title of ruler of the earthly realm. Essuel's mother was his father's concubine, a dragon queen from the outskirts of the solar system. His father fell in love with her power and her knowledge. A marriage would never have been allowed because she could only marry another dragon to carry on her legacy. Essuel is all that can represent their love. The father is forced to leave with the boy and unite with his arranged marriage to another queen who will birth Annuil.

Before Essuel and his father were forced to leave, the dragon queen taught the boy her craft. She showed him how to harness energy and create life within his own fingertips. An energy bolt can be tied into a knot and if a starseed is trapped within the coil, the energy is born into flesh. Essuel animates clay objects as his hobby. He practiced his human art with his mother before his exile. He continues his craft in the secrecy of his solitude, careful to hide his talent from his brother.

Essuel's illumination is slowly superseded by darkness because of the emptiness the young boy feels without his mother's love. After the wedding of his father to his new stepmother, Essuel runs away and calls for his mother. He misses his dragon queen and longs for her embrace of knowledge. He starves for her instruction, but she never hears his cries.

Annuil is born not long after. He is thrust into his brother's care without any forethought. Essuel's resentment grows because he knows the boy will grow to overcome him. Essuel cries for his lineage. He will be nothing but a soldier and will forever serve his younger sibling. It is at this moment the home of the Inogenue is reduced to terror and the family must leave and begin again on the welcoming aura of the Venetian paradise.

The father begins his mission to construct a terraqueous home for his family to live. He works day and night growing the tiny starseed into the subastral form. When it is finally complete, he takes his sons to the unchartered land. The boys worship the amazing sunlight tasting their skin. The brothers love the fertile ground. Essuel's father explains that the Earth is full of gold under the surface, and that the gold is made into the alchemy of desire that will one day restore the power stripped from the cosmos.

Essuel is left to lead the humans with the purpose to mine the gold. Annuil is left to educate and advise the people, careful not to let them experience the transformative emotions of love and hate. All is profitable for many years. The humans work the ground and the land is productive. The gold is passed to the father and he patches the voids of the universe with brilliance. For a moment in time, Essuel is distracted from the longing to be with his mother. Sad how quickly the empire will crumble under the covetousness growing between the brothers.

Essuel hates the unloving surroundings of humanity on the earth. His people should be able to experience bliss. He feels that they should experience the power and emotion of love as a blessing. He decides that he will make the people like him, to feel pain and joy, to love and hate. Essuel escapes to the other side of the world to hide from his brother's scrutiny. There he begins his mission to make a more perfect human.

Her name is Tonne. He watches her in the field with the other workers. She is different. Enlightened. Essuel knows she could be from another world, possibly even a being from the Inogenue. One day she is standing alone and he approaches her.

> You are different from the others. Your hair is
> blazoning red like fire. I have never seen such a
> color come from one's head.

Tonne is startled by this unknown man's exclamation to her. She studies his face. The man is large in stature, much taller than any human she has ever encountered. His vibrant skin glows with a golden aura flickering in the atmosphere. She knows that he is not human. He is something much like what she herself is.

> You are different too. Why are you so tall? You
> are like a herculean mammoth. Explain that
> occurrence to me.

Essuel stands back in retaliation. He is thrown from balance by
her counter attack. She has called him on his physique. Tonne
turns as she tucks her defiant strands of molten hair behind her
ear before walking away from him.

> Wait! Don't leave! I must ask you something,
> lady with the blazon hair. Do you want to know
> me as I do you? I want to show you what I am
> underneath this armor of gold.

Tonne stops walking. The urge to turn around overcomes her
need to leave. She walks back to him, stopping no farther than a
foot from his body. Essuel leans over her and smells the top of
her head, sweet and salty. He moves forward and kisses her
forehead, an act of protection.

> Come back here tonight and we will talk. I have
> a project and I think you will be what I need to
> complete my task. Will you come back here
> please?

Tonne smiles back at him and returns to her steps away from
him. Her curiosity is intrigued but her resolve forces her back
into the reality of her own secrets. Of course she is not of this
earth. She is the dragon. He watches as his future leaves. If she
is meant to help him with the Biolarity she will return.

Essuel can feel the starseeds longing to be one with her, to flirt
with her greatest asset, the beaming tendrils of fire that grow
from her head. He will exploit her trait for his own gain, not on
purpose, but it will be the result. His intent is masked with
sincerity; only time will allow the revelation of his true motive.

-IN THE BEGINNING-

The gabled entrance opens,
One death will surely find.

The Singularity has finally taken place. We stand alongside the machine. It is not computers as we thought would become us. It is the human that became the machine. We allowed the robot inside our bodies and the transformation has begun.

Never again will I feel. I will not cry, or even laugh. The only joy I get is to perfect my already beautiful home. Once it is complete, I will do it all over again. It is all I can do to keep up with the next guy. To be weak is to be already dead. I bought into this life of the condemned. I didn't realize it at the time of my fate because it is hard to see the devil when cleverly masked by the light of a savior. I want to be the best. I want to climb to the top of the ladder. How am I to know I will be jumping off into my own demise? It is only an imagined death. A nano cannot be killed. Death is not in the program.

The ones below, less fortunate and unable to keep up with the evolving technology, trickle off the top and become a malfunctioning living zombie. This is more than most can handle. I sit, virtually alone, now that Claira is gone. I wish I could join her but I can't end my suffering. I return to life, and with each return, I am mangled with the experience of a fragmented heart. I piece the jaded edges back together and move forward into the darkness that is my life.

My body is perfection, however, with no one to share my soul, it is pointless. I look at my skin and hair, all genetically cured of the disease of age. Although, my heart will be forever tortured with images of Claira choking on her own breath as she changed. I am jealous of her death, her freedom from this lifetime. It was a blessing to her that she did not live to see the sun expand. Now, all who are left cower below the fire. With the sun reigning as queen, we will all burn.

The nanotechnology has trapped me into a life I no longer wish to live. I wail into the night and scour through the day. She haunts my dreams, shadows my thoughts, and remains in my memories. My lovely wife turned to the dark stone we sought to avoid. I am alone in my regret.

I have become a gypsy with no home, a nomad with no cause. I left my world behind, the corner office and my once elaborate home, a life most would dream to live. Without her it is pointless and without these attachments I am free. How much debt must I pay to be released from this prison?

Ahead I see the infirmary, the next chapter in my story, a refuge for my empty soul. It is the place I have been advised will help me return to mental clarity. I want her image erased from my memory. Living with her stuck in my thoughts is torture and worse than any physical pain. I invite a new beginning within as I walk through the gates to my new existence.

+ + + + + + +

Jubrock stands in front of the heavy metal doors that lead to his safety. He knows that if the ones living below realize the truth of his survival, he will be tortured by their ignorance. The underground people fear his kind. He is the enemy. They do not know that he will deliver to them a message from the surface. Jubrock begins to knock but hesitates once more. Freedom is his illusion as he is bound by the responsibility she has given him. He takes in a deep breath and exhales as he pounds on the entrance with his clinched fist. He awaits a response.

Who is there? What do you want?

I am Jubrock. I have been sent to speak to Leerah.

The door opens and the tarnished wrinkled face of a man greets him. Jubrock enters the underground. As he steps across the threshold, he reaches into his back pocket and taps the book left in his keep, the word of her existence. The man pats Jubrock down and feels the book. He pulls it from the back of his pants.

> What is this? It looks like a handwritten journal. I will hand this to Leerah myself to see. Follow me to her.

> That book is not yours to share. I will give it to her if I choose to. You do not have the authority to....

> Oh but I do. You see down here you are nothing, but I am everything. She will want to know who you are before she meets you, that is, if you are wishing to join our colony.

> I do not wish to join your truncated group! I have a message to deliver to her from a friend, someone she will remember. That is all I want from your colony of delinquents.

The man looks at Jubrock hard in the face. He turns and motions him to follow down the corridor of the underground fortress. All around is sludge. Foul smells of urine and decay travel up Jubrock's nostrils tempting his stomach to empty. They stop at a door propped open slightly. Inside, a woman sits alone on a bed in the center of the room. She turns to look at the men. A patch, showing nothing of the injury behind, covers her eye. She stands and walks to Jubrock and smells his neck before speaking to her guard.

> Who is this man you have brought to me? He does not look like one of us. Have you checked his belongings? He smells...metallic.

> All he has on him is this book.

> Jubrock. My name is Jubrock.

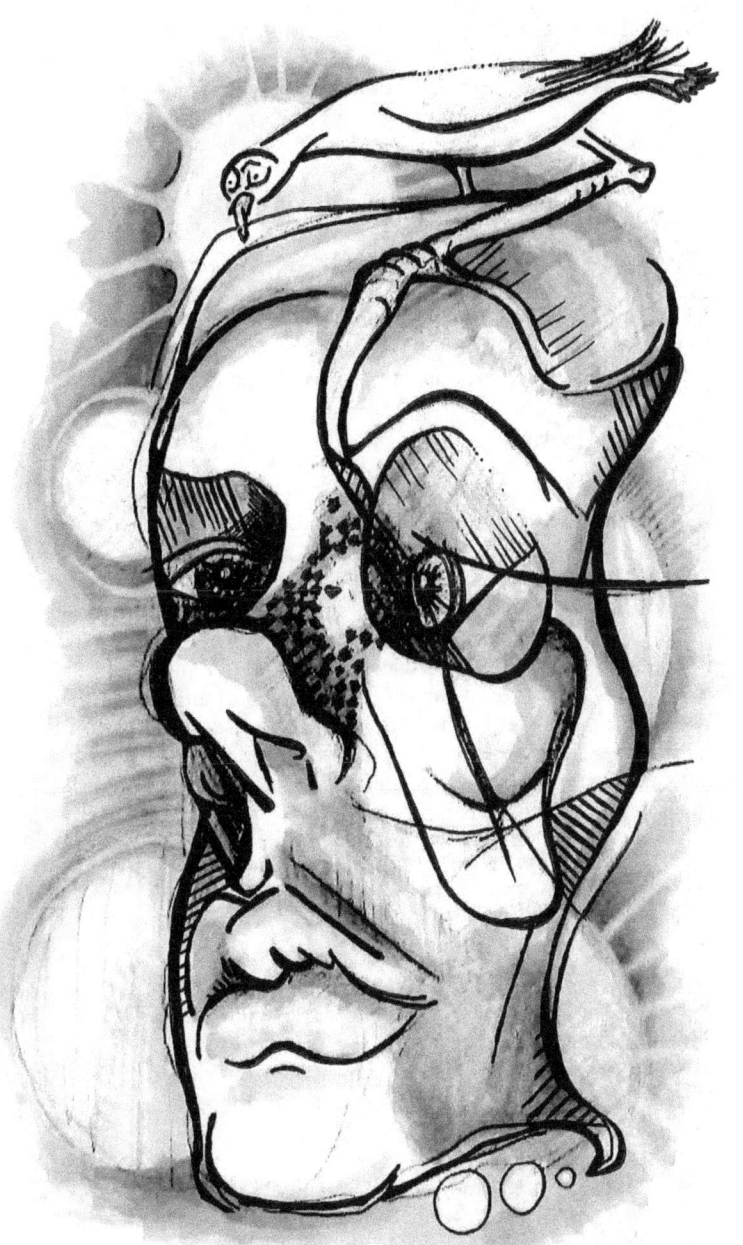

Leerah looks him over again through her remaining eye. She takes the journal and flips through the pages. She studies each passage trying to piece the letters together and make sense of the words. She instinctively knows the book belongs to her nemesis.

>Genue. Is she still alive?

>She is. She sent me to deliver a message to you.

>Oh yes. This I would love to hear. She will not speak to me in the face. I suppose she just can't stand to look me in the eye. Ha! I have but one eye thanks to her. Did she tell you what she did to my face?

>I don't know what history lies between you but I have to tell you what will be happening to the Earth on this day.

Leerah closes the book and throws it on the bed behind her. She steps back from Jubrock and looks over his form once more. He is built like a machine, muscles rippling under his shirt. The worn holes in his clothes reveal his tanned skin underneath. His black hair is slicked behind his ears. She looks deeply into his liquid eyes searching for the truth of his motive. He retaliates her stare and shifts the uncomfortable silence onto his other foot. She releases her visual investigation.

>Well, go on. I am curious to hear what the great Genue has for me to know. Like I would ever believe anything coming from her, but go on.

>There will be a fire that will make the way for the seed to grow once again. You will no longer cower beneath the sun as you have in this city below the surface. The phoenix will release her grasp and she will be consumed in the ashes of the past tribulation.

>Lies! You tell me these lies! The swollen sun is all we have known. It will never return. She sent you to confuse me didn't she?

Leerah stares at him. Blessed are the ignorant, unaware of the war raging inside, longing to release the dragon. She imagines the revenge she will have on the one who took her eye. Leerah will have her retribution. She will pluck the blue orb from Genue's tortured skull. She sees a use for this large creature of a man. He will lead her to Genue in exchange for shelter.

What exactly does this have to do with me anyway?

Jubrock looks at the scared girl in front of him. He tries to imagine the struggle she lives below the surface. All around him is the evidence of depression and heartache. The walls are crumbling around the room. Emaciated figures peer out of the corners, begging for substance to live another day. He feels pain in his own heart for what they have been through. Hunted for their organic flesh, the machine drives fear into their consciousness. This young woman holds the power to guide them into the future. She will be the one they trust. Jubrock feels the hate she holds for his perfect Genue. Before he can answer her question, the man who let him into the underground, returns panting from his hurried steps.

> Leerah! The doors are burning red! Do you feel
> the heat pouring in? There is fire all around. We
> must retreat further below the surface. We will
> not survive the heat even this far under.

> Gather everyone and take cover in the bellows of
> our camp! Lead the women and children first!
> Men, gather any food and water to carry with
> you! Seems this man is correct.

Leerah looks back once more at Jubrock before she leaves down the hall to escape the choking heat. He watches her disappear into the chaos of people running to hide deeper below the surface. He walks to the bed and retrieves his book. He sits and begins to sweat, bringing the book to his nose, inhaling the sweet flesh of the leather cover into his body.

The fire has begun. All above the surface will perish. He will await safety to return to his lovely Genue. His bond to the computer will allow his survival under the fire. Jubrock lays down on the bed, careful to tuck the book under his body. The sweltering fire pours in and his breath is snatched from his lips. He chokes under the fever of the molten air. His thoughts return to Genue. He thinks of her golden hair flickering above her like a crown. She will calm the fire and return the sun to balance within the universe. He is thrown into exhaustion and sleep overtakes his mind as the fire consumes his body.

-THE LEGACY WITHIN-

She draws it into her pores,
And drinks it through her veins.

Genue toddles around the kitchen holding her baby doll as she growls in joyful grunts and squeals. She is at the mental age to walk and talk in baby mutters. Physically, however, she is barely old enough to crawl at best, yet she walks and runs. The genetic transformations have created a superhuman. She sits on the floor and picks the tangles from her dolls matted hair.

Genue is the color of virgin white. Muted gold hues escape her skin and radiate through her aura. She emits purity. Yellow ringlets burst from her crown, shinning innocence compared to a cherub, as seen in the art of long ago. She is an angel sent to deliver Earth's existence from the destruction caused by the inflated sun.

Genue squeezes her doll to her chest. She looks around the room. Her eyes are the color of the sky on the brightest winter day, when the sun's blessing on Earth is reflected from its snow-crusted surface, trapped in the fog of moisture and blistering cold air. To describe her eyes, one must ponder; are they the darkest white or the lightest black? Genue evokes clarity. Though barely a toddler, she is mighty and must know, behind those eyes of crystal, that one day she will lead an army.

Her mother, Tonne, enters the room. Genue watches her, recording life happening in front of her, learning what one must grow to become. Tonne carries the burden of protecting this child. She was chosen to provide a life for Genue to grow. She must see that this child is raised to womanhood when her true blessing will show.

When the solar war began, and her world was destroyed, Tonne fled to the under-crust of society, the place where technology is rejected and where people crawl beneath the surface. They survive by the nourishment of the dirt and by the dripping of sunlight through cracks in the exterior pavement.

The sun is too close to survive in the atmosphere without an upgrade. The only people who can withstand the rays are *Enhanced Human Versions.* These humans have embraced nanotechnology and become specimens of this new science. With promises to alleviate the sun's damage, the Singularity is thought to be the answer.

People who can afford such drastic measures of living are clients of the *Nano-Clinic*. There, the microscopic technology is inserted into the body by vapors inhaled through tubes, placed deep into the lungs. The nano-robots then bind to DNA strands and immediately repair and regenerate all cellular structures of the body. People are instantly revived. Stress, exhaustion, and depression, all byproducts of a tortured body, dissipate into the nothing, as patients become a youthful upgrade of themselves.

All is well. The world prospers in the imagined safety of its own demise. However, as expected, the upgrades must be upgraded. Without the technology completed to remove broken and outdated nano-robots, the cadaverous foreign objects remain within the body. New computers are inserted, but like a virus, destruction spreads and the human body is malfunctioned. Upon the Nanotechnology crash, a zombie race is born. The belief that consumption of human flesh, untainted by the machine, would heal their gaping wounds began...

The hunt...the chase...the war

Tonne rests her elbows on the table across the room from Genue. She watches the little person sitting on the floor, holding her baby doll. Her abilities are still unknown. She is an experiment, the first of a race. Genue is the only being without nanotechnology who can withstand the sun's rays on her bare skin. Tonne tested this mutation when the baby was a few days old. She described the results in her journal.

I remember the crack in the ceiling, that when revealed would burn the hand of one without nano-cellular reconstruction. I walked the baby under the crack of decay and pulled off a piece of metal covering the enemy. Streams of molten light rays poured into the room.

Genue kicked her leg through the warmth. Her skin shimmered like amber syrup as she absorbed and digested the nourishing gift from above. I gasped in amazement! Genue seemed to glow. A deep blue aura radiated from her. She threw her head back and fell asleep in my arms as though she had eaten a meal. Nourishment from the sun, the air, the world around her, much like her genetic counterpart.

An impetuous discovery! I laid the baby in a wad of blankets and ran to the kitchen to retrieve a glass of water from the well reserve. I took the hydration into my mouth and sprayed it into the air around Genue. The mist floated around her and when she inhaled, the fog traveled into the pores of her skin. The water was absorbed into her. An astounding realization!

Biolarity is at once a functioning existence!

Tonne walks over to Genue sitting on the floor. The child reaches her arms up toward her mother. Innocence blossoms from her face.

Embrace.
The unknown.
Awaiting them both.

As Tonne holds Genue in her arms, she begins to cry. What will the days ahead bring? The responsibility of her mission weighs on her. The most important measure of safety is to hide, concealed from those who want her baby dead, protected only by the winter chill holding Genue's powers dormant. Tonne dreads the day the child will notice that she is different, the day she will want answers of how she came to be: her reason for living.

-The Toxicant Taste-

Truth be told, but never known,
In the rippled tale of lies.

The boy is startled awake. He looks out into the darkness of the room, allowing the familiar shape to concede him the illusion of safety. The pain travels up his arm and to his nerves, causing a ripple of the sharp sensation to move across his body. His mother places her hand over his mouth to silence the forthcoming cries. He knows it is her waking him from the darkness of his dreams, always in this same way.

She smoothens his coarse tendrils with her wrinkled fingers, coaxing him back into the land of nod. His eyes close and he begins to fall, disappearing into the collected consciousness, allowing the pain of her sting to penetrate the folds of his intellect, winding its existence into his dream.

His mother pulls the needle from his vein. The boy squirms under her grasp as she covers his disfigured body with a blanket. She says a small prayer for his soul, kisses her fingers and presses them against his forehead. She stands from the bed and exits his domain. His life matter is her salvation, her precious little secret. Pulling the door closed behind her, she walks down to the depths of her castle that lead to her fortress of solitude.

lips.
The words they
speak, the way
they feel.

Before thoughts have
reached them,
before anger escapes,

lips,
As laughter ignites,
to feed the hunger.

Through the lips,
her life is sustained.

In her laboratory, potions, concoctions, and a resulting tincture is made. She stares at the miracle created inside the liquid. His venom. She swirls the substance before taking it into her lips.

Heat permeates her cells. Sweat leaks from her pores and she begins to change. Her brittle shell fattens and her withered mask disappears. Her mind awakens and her eyes are wide to take in the beauty of her youth. She hears a startle behind her and looks to the direction of the commotion.

The boy looks at her and watches as she falls to the ground. He runs to help her back to her feet. Laughter escapes the confines of her form. Her beauty is returned, once again. Her deep green eyes diffuse the boy's confused stare. She stands, regaining her renewed composure. Taking his hand in her own, she leads the boy back to bed. He will want to know the truth. He will forever seek his mother's knowledge, wanting to know just how much his existence means to her.

Back to bed,
Now rest your head.
Dream in lies.
Live in lies.
Be of lies.
It is all a lie.
Now. Open your eyes.

The truth you seek to find lies within the tangles of the twisted web of lies. Beware of thy friend, your heavily disguised enemy. You will be cast into the role of the sinner's final act, judged, and ridiculed. Your final day will serve your justice.

The voice lingers in his dream and drifts along the folds of his intuition until the young boy is lulled back to sleep. His last thought is of the word PENANCE flashing in his sight. Then at once darkness falls and he is adrift in the unconscious psyche of the mind. Sleep, sleep my boy.

-THE TERROR OF THE PAST-

The sinful desire
of your callus nature.

Puddles of molten lava form and surround the chaos in a symphony of peace. At the core of passion she sits, the lovely Venus. Only a few rays of her blessing make it to the surface of Earth, however, within her heart, the Inogenue reside.

Essuel is now an adult, rebelled against his nature tribe, with his father at the brink of the discovery that the cosmos will be forever altered because of him. He watches the changing skin of the Mother Earth ship below. Venus sighs into the silence of the present condition.

The father places his hand on the soft surface of his home planet. He must show her that the love is not lost or she will throw the Inogenue from her paradise and send them back into the wasteland of space. The father glances at Essuel as he stands to attention, aged by the rebellion of his first-born son. The boy locks eyes into his father's stare and can feel his disappointment, and a dormant rage building within. The atmosphere around them swallows their disparity in an attempt to soften the blow.

> My son, my dear eldest son, your stubbornness
> has caused a great danger to our race. The
> dragons made a pact to kill our people. They
> sent her to seduce me. She took my innocence
> and passed her knowledge onto you. The
> starseeds are all we have, Essuel! Look around
> boy! They are now gone. You have harvested
> them into the human avatar and now we have
> no energy left. How do we survive now? I
> suppose when you wanted to defy me and
> create a new race not much thought was put
> into where this energy would come from. I am
> weakened. The dragons will come for my flesh.
> And after my protection is gone, they will come
> for you and your bride, Tonne.

Essuel gives his attention to his predecessor. Indignation, the
madness builds within his heart and it is hardened with the
passion of the Venetian paradise. She coaxes the boy into
restraint and he does not outburst. Control is his closest friend
now. He speaks calmly into the void of space.

> Father, you took my mother's innocence. I know
> the true Dragon Queen that you slander with
> words of deceit. I know what she is. I will never
> believe the hate you spread in her name. Nothing
> you say will ever change what she means to me.

A static ripples across the surface of the peaceful planet, jarring
their stance, sending her inhabitants to their knees for balance.
Venus is angered by the hatred spilling from Essuel's pursed
lips.

> You will hold your tongue boy for I am your
> Father! I dare not exploit your ignorance for my
> own gain! One day you will learn the truth even
> if it must be taught through treason!

Essuel looks to his brother standing on the other end of the
palace room. Annuil stares down at his own feet. He feels the
burn of his brother's eyes turned in his direction. Annuil told
their father of his secret studies.

And you, Annuil! Is this what you had in mind?
Now my karma is complete! You may have my
head as your justice. My brother, if you can take
it from my being, it is yours.

He bows down to his younger sibling in sarcastic disrespect.
Tonne looks at her love, her heart burning into Essuel's
withered resolve. She encourages him to continue his break
from the family of the Inogenue. Tonne welcomes the next
chapter.

I love them! I created them! Now you want me to
destroy them! Could you ever destroy your own
flesh? Could you turn your back to me as you are
asking me to do to them?

The silence is multiplied. Essuel stares at his father of stone; face
grumbled in the pressure to keep the peace. The father knows
more than his son and apprehends the human desire to rebel.
He knows that the humans will turn their back on the one who
has created them, to save their own life. The child is
reprimanded for giving the people the knowledge and the
passion of love and hate that will fuel the humans to grow into
a great army. The Inogenue will never survive their wrath. Only
this a father could ever know.

Essuel, you defied me. You gave them our
power. You gave them the very essence that I
forbade you to share. When I sent you to start
this project it was under the instructions that
they would not know the free will to love and
hate! I wanted them to know nothing and follow
our commands! Now they will surely turn
against us.

But I love them! They are mine and they are
perfect! I just wanted to make you proud by how
much better they will work the gold for us.

Shut up boy! You know nothing!!! You know not
what you have done. This is a disgrace to our
people. What about your brother? Did you think
of what he wanted from this?

Essuel looks toward Annuil. There was a time when they were so close, a time when they would talk all day imagining their own creations. Now that they have grown into young men, the drift has returned. Annuil has told their father of what Essuel did to the workers on Earth. He told their father of the lucent glow Essuel pressed upon their heads. The ripple he gave them, that flowed within the body as they became one with the light of the heavens and their eyes were cleared to see the truth.

> Now boy, you will stand back while I eradicate them. A great fire shall remove them from our presence and in time we may start the program again. This time your brother will lead the project. I am done with you!

Essuel watches as his father walks toward him. Hate rises through the son's veins. The emotional poison grows within, overcoming his existence, as he prepares his retaliatory speech.

> Father, who I have always followed and loved, I turn my back on you now. You must destroy your own flesh and blood to destroy theirs. I cast myself from your rule! I will not remain here and stand beside you and your insulting destruction!

Essuel turns away and begins the lonely walk from his father's love into the vast wilderness of solitude. Tonne watches him walk away. Her lover. She could never live without him.

> Essuel! Wait.

Tonne runs to him. She loves him. They created the people on Earth. Together they planned to reveal the program his father has in place to enslave the human race. Together they have planned to reveal the father's unjust nature.

> Tonne, you do realize you can never come back here. You will be exiled.

Essuel, we started this project together. We made this all happen. We will not stand back as he destroys all we have worked for. I will go with you to Earth and we will protect them together.

Essuel studies her face for a glitch as he touches her cardinal red strands of hair. He leans in and presses his lips onto hers. The passion of the kiss travels through their bodies. He wraps his arms around her and pulls her close.

Okay, Tonne. You are mine. They belong to us.

Tonne begins to cry and luminous teardrops escape her eyes, the precious golden tears of a Goddess. The father will miss them. Together they walk to the ship that will take them back to Earth, their mother ship. The war has just begun. The brothers will rival each other for the rule of the luscious planet.

In the distance, Essuel's father begins to blow toward the sun. He wraps his hand around his mouth as he exhales his breath and transforms it into a bolt of lightening. Annuil stands in support next to his father. He wants this fate. He wants them all to die. He wants Essuel to be punished for his lies and defiance.

Annuil watches his father propel the bolt of fire into the space of nothingness toward the Sun, the great ball of fire. It will grow with this nourishment and become too much for the precious terrain of the terrestrial sphere to handle, whose inhabitants will all die.

Tonne, it has begun! We must go to them and prepare the survivors of this catastrophe for the bloodshed that is to come. We will rise above him and overthrow him. He is tyrannical and has lost his love.

The war for the human kind has begun. The fight for the soul of man cannot be denied any longer. Essuel will return to his people on the Earth. He can save the ones who have been preparing for this. He has warned them before of the wave of fire that will serve as their Moirai.

-Juvenile Revelation-

Roaring gust of trepid wind,
Dismantle the path with friction.

The air is thick, in continual evaporation and precipitation, a constant fog by day and rain throughout the night. The sun leaches pools of water into the atmosphere. The resulting wet heat drains life through each passing breath. The remaining salt left on the beach, is tossed and thrown about in storms created by this constant flux of the weather. Fish and other water-life boil under the currents of the cyclical evaporating oceans, leaving behind a cesspool, unfit for consumption.

Those who walk above ground have become numb to the smells wafting in the breeze of the sewer air. Inside the cities, vacuums and purifiers have been constructed to help alleviate the water pressure and rid the stench clinging to the surface. This is the way of life. No one complains anymore. No one tries to lobby for change. It remains a constant reminder of the sun's powers and ultimate rule, having no mercy on the souls that crawl beneath her grasp. The sun does not consider those hurt by her rays of death, draining life, exhausting her welcome and leaving Earth no choice but to cower in her presence.

The outside is grey. All hues of the world around are muted to the color of a prison cell. The sun, a threatening fire, forces underground societies to crawl beneath the streets of abandoned cities inhabited only by the living dead, searching for clean flesh to consume.

Food is scarce and illness runs rampant. Burial ceremonies are held below in empty well taverns. Cremation and harvest of the resulting heat is used to power the societies below. A daily sacrifice of the weak and sick give life to those who remain. Only by the friendship of darkness can food be hunted and gathered by the survivors.

+ + + + + +

The time is now for the acknowledgement of Genue's TRUE powers. Tonight is the eve of her sixteenth birthday. Tonne has promised her an explanation for her abilities since the day the child began to notice she is special. Sixteen seemed to be an eternity away then.

> *My lovely Genue, on your sixteenth birthday, I will reveal the secret of your birth. You will be forever changed. Life as you have always known will diminish and a new, more dangerous one will take its place.*

Tonne walks into the closet of her bedroom. The dwelling is chalky and brown from dirt. Piles of magazines and papers line the curved walls of the room. Books, the only education that remain, are stacked beneath the dust, shelving the decaying memories, forgotten by the surrounding misery of life. She digs through her side pocket and pulls out . . . the key.

The key to the box.
The box that contains . . . the secret.
She opens the box.
Inside. . . the journal.

She drags her hand across the leather cover, tasting the warmth of the supple skin with her fingertips. Genue's origins are contained within these pages. It is the prophecy of her existence, her purpose, spelled out in scientific lettering. Others know of this book, longing to destroy the evidence of their nemeses, Genue. Those who hunt her will find her location soon. The winter blanket will soon recede to spring and she must be prepared for that day.

+ + + + + + +

Genue daydreams from her perch above the city. Today is different. She can feel a heaviness clouding within herself. Smoke dances out of the buildings in front of her. *Clutter, trash, and decay* are burned to create a dress to hide the sun. *Art, joy, and passions* are pumped through large chimneys. The fuel of life is now destruction. Fire consumes the *unnecessary, used, unwanted,* as the world is rid of *color, life, and existence.*

Genue looks down and notices a boy walking on the street below. She knows that he is human by the way his body moves. He is biologically untouched. This boy walks during the day. He scratches his arm. She leans in closer to see. His skin begins to smoke as he grabs his arm and turns to walk away, catching her with his eye. She flops her fingers through the air in an awkward salute. He backs up slowly and returns to the corner from which he came. Genue watches as the boy disappears. Are there more? Is she not alone?

Genue retreats back into the room and crawls down the length of the tower. She is the only one to be so far above ground, unknown to the others, besides Tonne. Her mother has promised her truth, now she must retrieve it. She climbs down the last staircase and is back into the safety of her community, down the barren hallway, past the elders gossiping. Women wash clothes, in vats of water like a slow-cooked southern gumbo. Small children stomp in the drips that escape the tubs. Genue glides by, unnoticed, except by a girl with soft brown dreads of hair, who looks up and smiles at Genue. Her innocence is contained in the unknowing of the world that once was, a world where humans were not trapped underground. You cannot miss what you never knew.

All hair is brown below the surface of the earth. No golden highlights, gifts from the sun, only brown. Genue must keep her yellow locks hidden beneath her cap. Often thought to be a boy, Genue uses this mistaken identity to her advantage. Her long, lanky body has not caught up to the idea that she is in fact a female.

Genue resembles the origin of her creation, a pure white orchid. Her lustrous gold tufts of hair bounce around her head like the voluptuous petals of the spectacular flower. Her crimson lips lead to the stem of her existence, feeding her soul. As her callow youth climbs to maturity, strands of auburn, the color of a warm flame, flicker from her scalp. She ponders the transformation.

Many changes have puzzled Genue over the years, wonders of why her eyes change color throughout the day and why water vapors are drawn into her skin. She thinks of how her outer shell radiates colors of blue and orange as she walks faster. The truth becomes closer to her intellect with the time. She approaches the door to her home. Three knocks. Four twists of the knob. The code. Tonne opens the door and Genue is wrapped in safety.

What did you see today?

Tonne helps Genue escape the sleeves of her jacket. She arranges the tousled hair released from the cage of the hat while smiling at the creation standing in front of her. Tonne knows that this day will mark the end of her duty to raise Genue. She will be released soon, as well as Genue from her. It is a moment of change for them both.

> I saw a boy, a biological boy, walking down the
> street. He had some kind of paint or something
> covering his skin.

Genue looks into Tonne's face for answers but finds nothing. She knows this uncomfortable silence. Secrets have plagued their conversations her whole life. All she receives in return is a blank stare. She continues her narrative, hoping to draw Tonne inside and reveal all that she may know. She wants truthful answers.

> His skin caught fire. He scratched the paint off.
> He then ran off and climbed into a dumpster
> around the corner.

Tonne's face is frozen. How can she hide this emotion creeping up her spine? They are looking for her daughter. At sixteen she will mature. They will smell her. They will see her. She is strong now that it is the eve of her blossoming. How can this reality be hid any longer? Tonne leans over the table, level with Genue's own eyes.

> This is important: we must leave this place.
> That…boy… is actually an evil man. He is a man
> that seeks to find you, who is concealed by a
> costume, a trick, to hide a monster.

Genue stares at her mother, full of questions, none of which she can summon to her lips. They must travel again. She notices the table between them and on it, the book. Her mother reaches her finger and strokes the warm cover as she speaks.

>This is the truth you wish to uncover. Among these pages tells the story of your conception, your existence and the purpose for your life.

Genue reaches for the book. She strokes her fingers across the soft surface, and then holds it close to smell the pages. She feels as though she is holding a relative sent to guide her passage. She welcomes this ancestor into her life and inhales deeply.

>Genue, you must protect the pages of this journal. You will die a traitor if they find you. Gather all you need to travel. We will leave when the sun sets and darkness rains over the sky.

Tonne disappears into the shadows to collect her life. Traveling has become routine. They must move with the seasons. Genue is camouflaged in a cloak of winter, diminishing her powers, in order to appear more human. It has been sixteen years. It is now time to travel into the flame, into the warmth. They must find the one who helped her escape before, when the Biolarity Lab was destroyed. The doctors did not succeed in finding the baby. She was hidden away and has developed into a young woman. Now the flame is all that remains.

Tonne has been preparing for the day of her release from the duty to protect the experiment, her daughter. She knows that Genue will need to use the heat from the sun to fully activate her powers. Tonne will cower to the majesty of the swollen luminary. Genue will walk alongside the molten queen, the ruler of their evolutionary path.

Underneath it all, don't forget who I am.

Genue opens the journal. The pages have yellowed with the passing days. She feels the parchment texture beneath her fingertips. Words dart around on the page as Genue wipes a tear from her face. Inside her story is told. Her purpose for life is detailed within the volumes of the journal. She smells the book once more taking the microbes into her skin, becoming one with the truth in front of her. She flips the cover back and reads the first page.

Biolarity Research Lab – Final Stage
Day one: Entry A
I have received the go ahead to begin the final stage of Biolarity. We have found the most effective genetic combination for the plant-human experiment: Angraeecum Sesquipedale: known as the Dancing Lady Orchid of South America. Family – Epiphytic (moisture and nutrients are absorbed through the air.) Characteristic physical attributes to the human form: Sensual, pale skin and hair, bright pink lips, nipples, hands/feet, and anatomy. Aura: Gold in the shadows or darkness of night and turquoise in the light of day, as though a cloud of mist protects the body from the costly elements of nature. After trials in the hologram machine, the orchid presents the most desirable plant properties to aid in human survival. Hypothesis: the Biolarity transformation will aid in the subject living upon the Earth without any use of nanotechnology. The subject will be able to ingest the sunrays as nutrients and collect any minute particles of water in the air for hydration. After trials using the DNA from each of the 83 families of epiphytic plant life, the orchid has been found to be a near perfect exact match, mainly due to the large surface area of the root. This allows for rapid absorption of water and nutrients from the air, resulting in the greatest chance of human survival. This is much related to the properties desired in human skin, to insure protection from ultraviolet rays. The human DNA donation has been derived through a female, of age 20. (Her file is included as Documentation 1, Entry A) Through the use of the Holographic Genetic Organizer, research has concluded that DNA of both subjects is a match. No observed abnormalities have been detected. Celebrations within the laboratory run rampant as our years of research into Biolarity now present a positive light at the end of a long tunnel. Transformations are scheduled to begin tomorrow, as tonight we will feast to commemorate the final stage of study: Conception.

Genue gasps. Conception! Conception of what? An idea? A project? Not a human, a plant person. She fumbles through the pages searching for the file, Documentation 1. It must contain answers. She finds it torn in half. Only the basic demographics are listed; red hair, a trait that is nearly extinct. She searches the pages for a date, nearly twenty years ago this all occurred. Genue stares into the muddy ceiling as if the answers are written on it just for this occasion. Lost in the folds of synopsis, flickering with the electrical current, she thinks.

Am I a plant? Am I even human at all?

Tonne reemerges from packing in her room. She glares at Genue frozen in the chair, deep in the delirium of thought.

Are you ready? Where is your traveling gear?
Come on! Read that later. You will learn more
than you ever wanted in time. Right now we
must escape to find safety.

Tonne rushes into the kitchen and throws open the cabinets to collect herbs and dried seaweed, the only plant lettuce left on Earth. Genue closes her book, the topic of her obsession, and slides it into her bag. She puts on her hat and bandana for the massive sand storms, goggles and chain mail gloves, for protection. Her jacket: back on. She works her leather chaps over her pants. Then her steel toe boots. Her belt hangs by the door awaiting their departure.

Genue throws her bag over her shoulder and is joined by her mother. She adjusts her belt and buckles it in place. A quick check of her pockets for the contents: knife, two flint rocks, and chapstick. Tonne looks at her daughter, the warrior that will take on the salvation of the world.

Darkness invites itself into the solitude of her surroundings. This will be the last time Genue will pass through these doors of her underground prison. The journey begins as it has so many times before. She releases her fear of the unknown and invites the welcoming arms of change into her life. She knows she is different than the others and that her mother has taken great care to protect her from the dangers that await her.

+ + + + + +

Edextrous. Can you hear me?

He can hear her words as they stir within his unconsciousness. He jerks his avatar of fantasy free and returns to the realm of reality. He is awakened. Emila sits in front of him. He stretches his neck toward her hand as she runs her fingers through his hair, gliding her touch down the enlarged muscle in his neck.

> The shock from the heat threw you, but we did it Edextrous! We created the life. The bud has formed. So far the experiment is following our hypothesis.

That would explain the glaring pain to the back of his head. Dr. Edextrous collects his constitution. Standing to his feet, he stumbles to the incubation tank at the end of the room. The Biolarity project will be the answer to his lack of career. For years he has watched as his fellow classmates graduate school, accept grants, and residencies. It is his time to introduce his answer to science. He will discover the antidote and will hold the power. The serum of the Biolarity, pumping through his heart and powering his brain, will make him a superhuman. Inside the glass tank two flower buds pulse their petals, growing in the artificial light. The doctor leans in close to study the life emerging within.

> Emila, we have merged the DNA! I mean that this thing we have created is alive. It will grow into something. We may only have days before the human characteristics begin to surface.

The doctor circles the tank and stops, looking at her in disbelief. He walks to Emila and takes her face in his hands. He kisses her lips as she wraps her arms around his waist.

> Maybe this will please him and satisfy his hunger.

-The Enemy's Lodge-

I lit the spark,
That you set aflame.

> I have returned, however, I am alone. She was
> not at the given location. The underground
> compound was ambushed but we could not
> find her.

The misfortunate words are spoken to the back of
the sunburned flesh of his worn leather chair. His hand is
revealed, as he strokes the arm of his throne. Long knobby
fingers dance above the aged cracked surface.

> I told you not to return without the girl, you
> stupid machine. I can't believe that you even
> come back here to tell me this.

The root-like fingers reach forward and push a button on the
chair arm. A trap door opens beneath the stupid excuse for life.
Death welcomes his arrival.

> Insignificant! Insubordinate! Incapable! I gave
> simple instructions. Don't come back without
> the girl. Simple. And he came back without the
> girl. Stupid.

The monster stands, untamed tresses surrounding his head, and walks over to the window. His black coat drags the floor, flapping with each passing step.

> How hard is it to follow a simple order! Bring that girl or never return. JUBROCK!!! Come here!!!

In walks a beastly creature, clutching his tool belt, boasting his implements of torture. Jubrock is at once called to the attention of his master. He knows he must produce a body. The evil one speaks often of the girl, the one who is better than him. His jealousy and resentment have led him to hunt for her head.

> Find the one who looks like me! Or don't come back!!!

He turns toward Jubrock and the villain's face is revealed. White, sick, pasty skin, gnashing teeth and bright red eyes stare back at him. The miscreation walks back to his throne and sits, reaching his twisted fingers to pick up the journal, his mother's words, containing the details of his dejected life.

Sathe. His name is Sathe, with his crystal blue eyes, blond barbarian hair, and pale lifeless skin. He wears a long black coat to hide his difference and carries a small metal box that contains his boost equipment. He has combined nanotechnology with his Biolarity mutations to create wings that spread far out above his body. This addition is done as an attempt to heal his distorted figure. Sathe is the one behind the forces to kill Genue. He knows that she escaped the fire. He is also aware of the prophecy told.

Sathe is smooth. When he smiles he licks his teeth. He will suck the blood of humans to restore his own balance. After he ingests life into his empty core, color is restored to his flesh. His eyes are shot with violence and his poisonous soul is rotting with hate and infirmity.

He has his mother's journal. She gave it to him before he killed her. She was hiding his secret written within the pages. His sister will destroy him and the world that he has created. Sathe opens the journal to the page of most interest to him, the one chronicling his fate and intention for life, scrawled in her arrogant lettering. It is the detailing of his story. His purpose: unwanted. Sentenced to death. Enslaved by her. He reads her judgment held within the pages.

A male. The first creation is a male. I don't understand the rationality behind this. The DNA donated is from a female. I always had doubts that this would not work. Against the advice from the Board, the moneybags still wanted a male.

When the DNA from the donor and the orchid were fused, his plant mutations did not recede below the surface of his skin. The orchid dominates, causing his human form to become the recessive gene. His skin is an iridescent green. His nails on both fingers and toes grow into a root-like point. His head resembles the human form, however, it looks closely like the bud of a plant. His hair comes out in course branchlike dreadlocks. His crystal blue eyes pierced my curiosity and melted it into longing. He smiled at me today with his profoundly crimson lips, still just an innocent babe.

Due to the nature of the joining cells, we now have proven that at this point, a female is the most desirable outcome. The doctor ordered the termination of the male experiment after the successful creation of the female. She is perfection. He is not. Of course now they see what I tried to warn them of before this all began.

I offered to carry out the termination myself. They released the baby to me in a wooden box with holes cut out along the sides. I couldn't imagine why there would be air holes. Wouldn't suffocation be more humane?

The process of termination is electroshock in a bath of saline and water. The substance to support life is used to destroy. I am sickened. As I walked down the hall to the death chamber I felt a wave of empathy for the small creation, the life I helped create. So I left with him. I brought him home and now I am at a loss of what to do.

He screams into the night and I can't make him stop. When he cries a green mist is released from his pores. I dare not touch him to soothe his pain. I watch him. I cry for him. While they celebrate her life I mourn his. How long will I be able to sustain him? When he sleeps, I am relieved. I feel that I am at once peaceful. Sometimes I feel that it would have been better to end his life, to end the suffering even before destruction had a chance to begin.

They celebrate her creation. The girl. She will provide a link to a new future for all of humanity. Once her life matter is studied and stabilized her soul will be sold off piece by piece to the affluent ready to pay money for survival. Her life will be slaved way for the continuance of theirs. I am sickened to have been a part of this. I wonder what will happen of me and this rejected science experiment, the twisted freak not suitable for study, the monster I have taken on as my own responsibility. I feel that my heart is too big and my patience too small. Now I will rest for a new day brings deeper turmoil.

We are watching and we know he is with you.
Through his hatred and anger he will rise.
Against our true wishes
she has been created,
to do that which you were unable,
in order to save what he
intends to destroy.

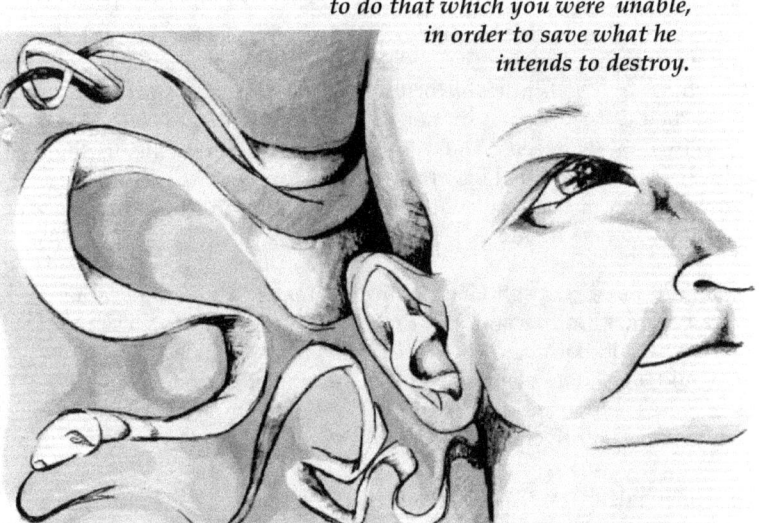

Penance is due to the one who fuels the fire............

-Discovery of a Twisted Perception-

Like the phoenix at the end,
Will burn it down and start again.

Annuil looks into the vast nothingness of the universe. It is pointless without his brother. Since Essuel has left the father has become ill. He stays in a constant fluctuation of sadness and self-inflicted torture. He stood aside as his father set the destruction into motion, the devastation that is intended to free the starseeds and return them to their home in the heavens. He fears that his brother's stubbornness will lead to his own death. Essuel will not leave his colony on the Earth. He will try to save them.

Annuil must choose to side with his great and powerful father or help his brother and join their forces to overthrow his rule. They would both be thrown from the graces of the heavens and would live their eternal lives on the planet of their captivity below. The twisted dagger of his decision stabs at his confused and wilted resolve.

Cemented in the trap between his father and brother, Annuil throws himself to the floor. The agony of his fate is spiraling within his thoughts, torturing his rational cerebral wavelength, causing the static to ripple.

I cannot breathe! Mother! Mother please come help me. He is choking my consciousness into the nothingness! Mother!

Annuil rolls on the cold floor crying into the harsh stone. Why would his brother ever leave him and take the girl instead. She is responsible for their separation. She came between them and took his attention away. She thrust it upon herself, stealing his gaze.

Annuil! Annuil! I am here. What is wrong with you, my son?

Mother, I am loosing my grip! I am falling from the edge of my torment. Why must father kill Essuel? Can't he just have the land and his people? We can all live in some way all together in this vast galaxy!

The mother looks at her son. Visions of her sweet child, she has watched grow these years, pass through her mind. She has observed him be berated and pushed around by his older sibling, yet he still worships that being. He forgives each atrocity like it will be the last. This painful blow is occurring now after Essuel has left their world.

Annuil, you will not understand the sacrifices your father has made to give the world to you. He has chosen you to be the ruler and Essuel will never understand the reasons for it. Your father's sudden collapse is the result of the urgency to intervene in your brother's sinister plan. My caring and trusting son, he trapped those souls in an avatar of flesh. That is not right. Our own macrocosm will darken and loose it's will to fight. Once the light is gone, the power will go out. This must be done or we will all succumb to the emotion of darkness, fed by fear.

Annuil stares into his mother's eyes. He knows she speaks the truth. She is the only one who has ever held any authenticity to his life. His brother enslaved the starseeds into the human purgatory. All life forms have the potential to become one with the Earth. If the fire is not in existence, the soul will break in half. Most have never made it to that point.

Each starseed plays a piece in the game as they travel in clusters and make a united decision to come to the Earthly being. Agreements are made and locks are given keys, then the soul will disappear into the womb of life, starting the journey of time within the three-dimensional plane.

Starseeds do not know their memories while in the physical realm. The focus is to find the one with whom you have made the agreement of love. You cannot settle for the comfort of it all. Knowing that passion is most uncomfortable, you continue on the journey. The only way to know oneself is to keep the company of no one, however, it is a lonely, comfortable feeling. Then you see her. Her razor eyes cut the tension of your stare. She smiles, twisting a tangle of hair with her hands; her touch, soft and gentle, like a porcelain doll. She is to be studied with great care.

At once the dream is shattered when she falls for another. Tonne never looked at Annuil the way she did Essuel. Her calescent hair thrashing in the fiery Venetian atmosphere as her feelings of infatuation take over all rationality. She is lured away by Essuel's charm, his watery seduction of the mind, the intensity of the night in one touch. Essuel is passion and Tonne is embedded. Annuil sits in silence once more as he has done so many times before.

Unrequited love is the most uncomfortable of feelings. He waits for his moment to wander back into her view, once Essuel is gone. Annuil smiles to himself, licking his teeth, a habit that has become most comfortable to him.

-Captive Adolescence-

Through winter vigil never break,
her frailty not shattered.
The other who wishes to take,
A supreme gift from above. All is at stake.

The forest of crippled trees sway in the sauna air and dance in the sweat of the night. Tonne and Genue rest after the long travel. They will not be able to move in the daylight because Tonne will fry under the sweltering heat of the sun. She pulls out her thermal blanket and crawls beneath it for her sleep.

Genue sits on the ground and digs her hands into the sand. The heat of the Earth travels through her fingertips warming her overworked muscles. She reaches into her bag and pulls out her journal. She carefully fumbles the pages of the aged manuscript.

Biolarity. What does this have to do with her?

Genue studies the passages closer and finds a page with a newspaper clipping taped inside. Below the article is a picture of two people standing in front of a building. The lady looks familiar. She brings the page close to her eyes. *'Emila'* is sketched below the image in pencil. Has she seen this woman before in person? The familiar washes over Genue's memories as she tries to place the woman's face from her past.

Tonne would have the answers. Her mother would know how they met. If she can pull the truth from within the twists of deception, all could be solved within the ripples and folds of her mind. Strange occurrences through the years with so few explanations have filled the empty space of her exceptionality. The frustration of not fully knowing who she is eats away at her confidence. Is she only worth enough to be hidden away from others who may be like her? She reads the article beneath the picture.

Biolarity:
Science of New Beginnings,
Or a Backtrack into the Past?

A new science, Biolarity, began by ODSA to create life on the moon, has found a new purpose in the world of science - Cellular Regeneration. Dr. Edextrous Shaw and lead scientist, Emila Brion, head a team of 17 fellow scientists of the genetic mutation field into this breakthrough study. If successful, Biolarity will provide a more natural alternative to the booming Nanotech industry. The catch? Plant DNA. Coverage of this emerging science will be provided and offered to the public seeking answers for combating our greatest threat to date – Solar.

Upon closer inspection of the building in the background, Genue reads the sign over the front entrance. -*Biolarity Lab #1, 2039 Avenue of ODSA*- She can find this place and see it for herself. Genue closes the journal. She feels the sandman entering her present condition. She rubs her eyes and displaces the dust before it can settle. She looks over at Tonne, already asleep, exhausted from the journey.

Genue is now sixteen. Adulthood is closer to her than childhood. She smiles at the quiet skeleton tree above her as she lies back on her bed of dirt and daydreams about her future. Peace washes over her mind and body as she drifts into a deep trance. Truths are to be revealed, within the psyche, at a time when it is least expected. A dream washes over Genue's unconscious thoughts. She feels the closeness of her ancestors wrapping her in a welcoming embrace. She feels at home within the thoughts inside her solitude of imagination.

Once Genue is contained within the safety of her subconscious intellect, she is free to explore the suppressed memories of her cellular structure. She sees a garden of knowledge all around her and the vines of synopsis pull her inside, enveloping their leaves around her, swaddling her innocence with their protection. The orchid, her relative, is now a part of her story. She sees the connection of the plant to her past and evolving future.

In the distant folds of her dream she sees a static ripple around the orchids and then it begins to disappear. All Genue can feel is the white nothing all around her. A grey cloud approaches overhead. She does not fear the storm that is coming closer. A message repeats in her mind. She listens closely as to not miss the most important point of her hallucination.

-Inogenue-

I am the Inogenue. Light. Darkness. Space. Forever.
I was sent to make it possible for your existence.
You are not of this earth, but you are here to save it.
Your existence was created with flame.
Explosion. Heat. Passion.
Your life will engulf the sun and you will be nourished by fire.
The humans will survive and the planet will begin to heal.
With your service, you will be free, our final gift to you.

Genue watches in her dream as the light drifts into the depths of her deepest delusions. Flashes of bright light: White! Blue! Pink! She blinks as she is awakened by the sudden realization that she is not alone. Genue knows that she is no longer within the safety of her dream. This is real.

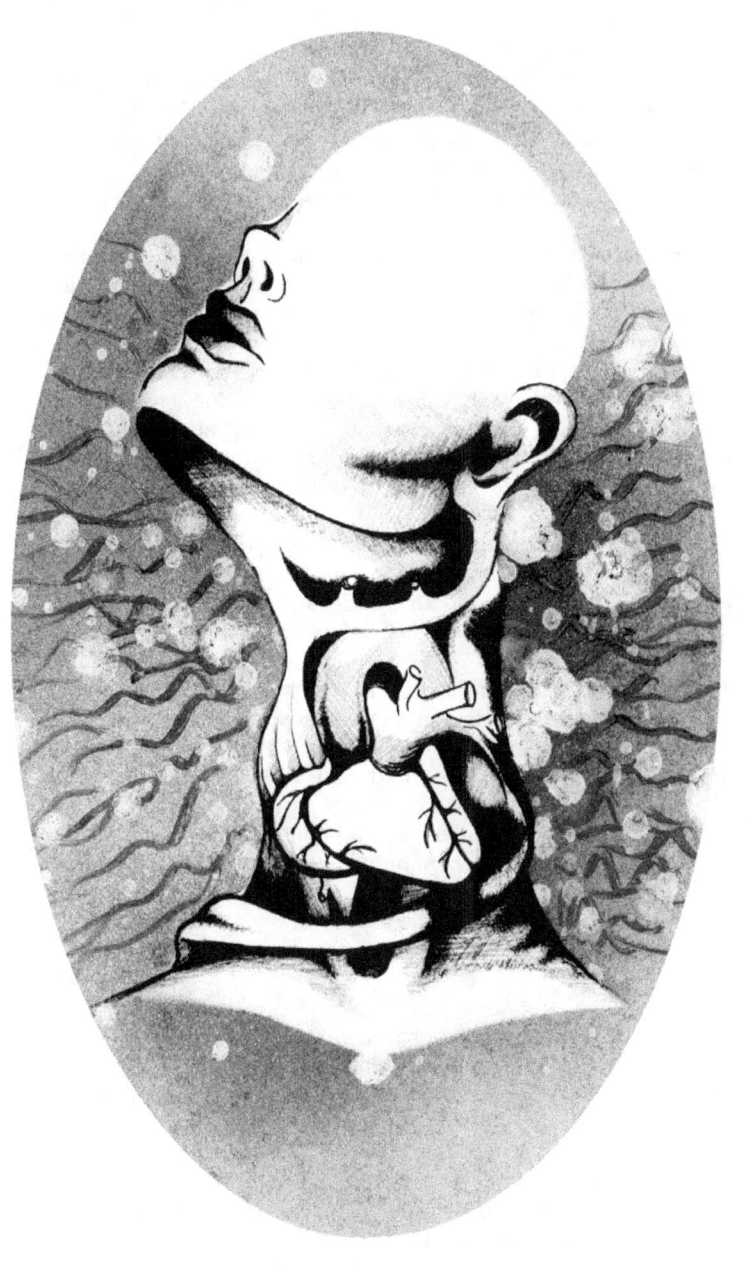

Genue feels his presence around her. She can see him now as he stands above her body. It is the boy from the street. She notices the black scab covering his arm where the sun licked his flesh. He leans in closer to Genue's face and smiles, allowing his yellowed, decay of teeth to shine. Splashes of green matter saved inside crevices of rot stand in attention for her inspection.

A troll. Her mother was right. He is no boy. The thick coating covering his skin is not paint as she thought before. It is a thick sludge from the grotto below, a hard crust of filth and stench that protects his shell from the swollen orb of fire. Genue pulls herself up from the ground, her lanky frame towers above his own squat stature. She slowly reaches to the ground and retrieves her belt. Buckling it around her waist, she realizes that Tonne is no longer there. She looks around with frantic emotion.

> Tonne! Mother! Where are you?

> Oh. . . I done took her back to my camp. I spose
> you just got come back wit me.

The troll strokes his matted chest hair peering out from under his vest. He licks his lips at Genue. Stepping closer to her, he eyes his tasty morsel. Genue is numbed with disbelief. Tonne has been captured. It was the dream, with such a depth, that masked her reality and she could not perceive the struggle. She remembers the Inogenue. He takes her lifeless arms in his scabbed hands and ties them tight behind her back.

> Got one pay high price fo yo head. Yo can tink
> o me as a. . . hunta o sorts. A hunta wit me
> prey.

The ogre man examines his handiwork of knots before pushing Genue ahead of him. He pulls out a stick from his tool belt and pops her on the arm with it to encourage her obedience. She begins to walk.

> Naw yo betta go on wit no troubles. Yo not
> wont me to take out. . . me anga. . . on yo
> partna. . . naw do ya?

How is she here? They were to be at the night's edge by now. That dream. Inogenue. She taps the back of her belt. Beneath her pants, she feels the edge of her journal. It is safe for now, however, she may not be.

Through the fog she can see a tunnel ahead. No words. She keeps hers inside. He babbles constantly. Genue can only decipher pieces of his dialect. She has never encountered such a strange language variation. They reach the entrance to the depths of her approaching hell, her captivity for now until she is sold to the ONE.

The troll pushes her ahead into the entrance of her confinement. He slams a gated door behind them trapping her inside his secret. Through the darkness, she is guided down a path. Genue can feel the dampness of the air around them. She deeply inhales the moisture into her body and she drinks the molecules into her flesh. Genue can see a cavern ahead of them. She can feel that Tonne is near. Once inside, she can see the shadow of a crumpled figure mangled into a ball on the harsh concrete floor.

> Tonne! Tonne, wake up! Can you hear me? We are found!

> Shut up girl!

Genue turns to the troll at the same time the metal pole swings into her skull. Shock travels fast down her spine, plunging her to the ground. A deep sleep overtakes reality as she is thrown from her cerebral thoughts and into the vast nothingness that is her pain.

-AWAY FROM THIS DOOM-

The world falls to his feet,
As he steps inside the destruction of reality.

Slap. Slap. Slap. Annuil walks down the corridor, black cloak slapping the heels of his boots. He stops at the entrance. Once he passes through these doors he will forever be owned by the underworld. He takes a deep breath to release tension from the confines of his tortured brain. He savors the cold of the alloy surface with his fingers. He was told to come here by his mother, his adviser.

Annuil knows she means no harm and only wants her son to take over their cosmic realm. He will be her flesh that will rule the stars. He takes one last breath before entering into the beginning of his greed for power. His fall has begun.

Once on the other side, he is within the computer. Pulsing heat licks his skin, tasting his sweat as he walks the parameter of the room, a mainframe, the nucleus of evil. His brother's project of domination lies here.

Hello there. Are you looking for the doctor?

Annuil spins around to see a squat man standing behind him. He contemplates the question. He does not know who he is looking for but this is a start.

> I am here for the one in the know. Are you following me here? I was sent to retrieve something. Are you Edextrous?

> I am not. I am just a student. But I can take you to him. Are you interested in the Biolarity project? You know that is what the brilliant doctor has been working on. Came to him suddenly one night. Then he built this holograph machine. Said the plans were given to him in a dream. Insanity, if you ask me. Plants will save us from the sun. That is just unbelievable!

Annuil follows the chattering man through the building to the doctor's hiding place. Incoherent nonsense spills from his mouth, however, they fall on deaf ears. Annuil does not care for words. He waves his fingers across his own lips and blows in the direction of the man and his words are at once silenced.

> *For a moment I can think. I know more than he could ever comprehend. My deceiving brother created the Biolarity program. He created the antidote to my machine in order to destroy my father. What a fool's dream. I have come here to shake his core. The doctor will crumble. He will fall and I shall catch him and enslave his Biolarity. I shall have Tonne, and Essuel in turn will pass into the nether.*

Annuil smiles to himself as he thinks of the future ahead. They stop in front of a double door. It has a sign that reads: Incubation Room. Annuil pushes the door open, letting himself in without invitation, and shuts the nosey man out. There is no need for his blank stare of confusion. No one will ever understand the workings of the Inogenue. A mere mortal may attempt to comprehend them but they will always fail to unlock the enigma.

Edextrous! Oh Edextrous! I know you are cowering in here somewhere. Where is the boy? You know all I really ever wanted out of this is the boy. I allowed you to make the female but I get the boy! I have come for answers, Edextrous! Where are you?

Annuil thrashes around the room throwing papers and knocking over tables. He blows into his hand and a flame curls out from his fingertips. He walks by a bookcase and drags his fingertip inferno across the bindings, igniting the scene and encouraging the incandescent destruction to take over. A tall man of medium build appears from the other side of the room.

Stop this madness! I am here Annuil! I am over here…

So glad your cowardice allowed for your arrival. Where is the experiment? I have come to collect what is mine.

The boy was incinerated. He was poisonous. We could not let him….

What have you done? You have killed him! I do not believe this! I will not allow this to go on without the boy. Either he is my payment or I will take the girl instead.

Annuil, don't even think of taking her! Her fluids are not poisonous. You will have no use for her.

I will take her only to destroy what you have worked so hard to create, Edextrous. I don't care about the Biolarity or even if it saves these humans from their death. I want them all to burn. I want them to die. Those human creations are my brother's project. Where is Tonne anyway? I feel that she is still here. I know she must be in recovery after donating such a large portion of her DNA to this project.

Edextrous looks at Annuil, not understanding how he knows of Tonne, her name is unknown to him. Her information is confidential. He feels the tug of a twisted perception rattle inside his mind. At once Edextrous realizes who Annuil is within the grand scheme of it all.

> Remember, I know all. I created this whole existence that you humans like to claim. And I also know the boy is still alive. Bring him to me or I will destroy both females of this project in the name of *Casualties of Science*!

Without another word Annuil disappears. Edextrous falls to his feet and sobs into his folded arms. He pulls his glasses from his face and throws them across the room. The blackness of his empty soul infiltrates his being and he is left alone with the monster of his darkest emotions. This wasn't supposed to happen. When he agreed to do Biolarity he wasn't intending for the experiment to be disfigured. Now they will take the girl instead. They will take the precious one: his precious one.

The doctor slips into a dream toiling and turning inside his tenebrous affliction. Sleep is his only comfort, his only escape from the reality of what is to come.

Annuil will return for the girl. He will take the orchid child in spite of Essuel. He also knows that the doctor has been working all sides of the situation for his own benefit and for that he will surely die. The doctor drifts into a coma. In the physical world, the collected consciousness is ignored. Upon entering the hyper-reality of thoughts, physical space is expanded and the possibilities of neural exploration have no bounds.

+ + + + + + +

Emila moves a hair from his face. She has returned to the lab and has discovered Edextrous asleep on the floor. He awakens to her touch, eyes darting around the room piecing together the puzzle of reality. He gasps at the weight of his present condition. He takes Emila's hand in his as he slowly speaks to her.

There is something you must know about Biolarity. I did not create this science. I was visited by a phantom; a spirit-like being explained to me that he had fallen from the grace of his father in order to save mankind. He told me that the only way to protect our people from the destruction of the bloated sun was to create a plant/human hybrid to absorb the rays. I made a deal with the devil that day and I feel my *penance* tighten its grip.

Emila sits back on this new information. She tries to imagine a superior race to her own humanity. She thinks of all they have done in the name of Biolarity and now she knows it was all a lie to her. He told her what she needed to hear and now the plan has gone wrong.

Why are you telling me this? I have followed you on Biolarity from infancy to our successful creation of the female subject. You instructed me to kill the male. Why was he even created!

Emila, all things in this ethereal realm must have a balance between good and evil, love and hate. He was created as an antithesis to her purity and goodness. We had no use for him after that. The Inogenue will return for their formulations. They will return for what we have created in their structure, containing their inherent powers.

What do you want from me Edextrous?

I want you to hide the girl and her mother. Hide them away for sixteen years. That is when my contract with the beast will expire. The baby will be mature at that point and her potential will become relevant. She must be protected. The mother is one of them. Her red blazon hair is alien to our own culture. She must never learn of her true being or she may reunite with them.

It will be done. I will hide them away and clean up your mess, Edextrous. The female orchid child and her mother will disappear tonight.

+ + + + + + +

Emila wakes from her dream. She is covered in sweat. Who knows that she took the boy? She grabs her robe and runs into the other room where he sleeps. How could he destroy anything? She sits on the chair beside his bed. **She will save what he intends to destroy.** The voice pounds inside her mind. An idea immerges from the depths of her frustration. Emila thinks of a plan to incinerate the Biolarity facility. This realization relaxes her and she slides back into her bed of dreams.

Emila returns to the lab the next day as she has done so many days before. She watches Genue sleep inside the incubation tank. The tiny seed has sprouted into a human form, one that exactly resembles the boy hidden at her home. Tears stream down her face, knowing the fate of the plant creations haunt her thoughts.

If the study is successful, the fluids and DNA from the girl will be drained and harvested for the consumption of the elite as an alternative to the destructive nano-robots. This will be done in order to live in harmony with the sun. The elite do not ask questions about where the cure comes from. They do not care that the growing plant-human will spend her days sedated and hooked to a machine with tubes draining her body of life.

Emila wipes her tears. Death is a blessing to the growing soul trapped by existence. She leaves the room and walks down the hall to the recovery room where Tonne sleeps. She is the one who gave a piece of her structure to create the tortured lives of the two experiments. Recovery is a long process for her.

The DNA was removed from the tissues in her spine in order to obtain the richest specimen. She is young, in her early twenties, still a child herself. She has become tangled in these lies of doing for the better good. Her fine sanguine red hair, a trait extinct in human genes, spills over the side of the hospital gurney. She is an anomaly of these days, however a perfect match for the orchid. She was placed within the physical realm with a purpose to create the Biolarity.

Tonne opens her eyes and looks at the familiar face in the room. It is Dr. Emila, the lead scientist and the brains behind the whole operation. Tonne can feel something different about her visit today. Emila cannot destroy the life of the female specimen she helped create anymore than she could the male. She walks over to Tonne and stands her up onto her feet. Confused and unable to speak, Tonne questions Emila with gestures and made up sign language. Emila speaks into the space surrounding them.

> Don't be afraid of what is about to happen. Things are strange now. Be strong and do exactly as I say and you will survive.

Emila fumbles her jacket off her own back and onto the weakened woman. Tonne stumbles under her grasp. She must build her sea legs for the journey ahead. The doctor frantically searches the room for the patient's few belongings. Tonne points to a hook behind the door holding her bag. Emila grabs it and digs out her driver's license.

> I will hold onto these so I can find you later. Now listen closely, Tonne. I will take you down the hall across from the incubation room. There, I will give you a box. Open it only after you are far from this place and in complete safety. Take this file. Inside are instructions on how to care for what I am going to give you. Do not get caught. Do you understand? I will follow you and reveal myself to you at a later time.

> *Confusion. Exasperation. Is this a dream?*

Emila leads Tonne down the hall and pushes her toward the incubation room. She walks, taking each step, as if it is her first, stopping to lean onto the wall for support. Emila disappears behind the large metal doors, leaving her alone in the hallway. The door opens, once again, and she places a wooden box in Tonne's arms. It is heavy with holes drilled in the sides. She holds the box tight against her chest knowing there must be life inside. Emila digs out a roll of cash from her pocket and shoves it into Tonne's bag.

> Leave through the back doors. Everyone is gone for the night so no one should see you. Don't look back and if you are ever questioned, you don't know anything. Okay?

Tonne tries to nod her head in response but Emila has already shoved her further down the hall. She turns to see the crazed doctor disappear back into the room. Loud crashes! Glass shatters, falling to the ground. Afraid of her new reality, Tonne tries to run. Her feet seem to be magnetized to the ground. The door is ahead. She pushes the lever and releases herself into the darkness of the night. Escape, or imprisonment, she does not know. It doesn't matter anyway. It means the same thing in the cycle of life.

The obscurity of the night atmosphere welcomes her into its company. She knows she must hide this treasure away. Tonne walks to a bench on the edge of the parking lot and rests her wasted body. She holds the box close to her chest. She already knows what is inside. The sweet smell of an innocent baby drifts from the holes and into her nose. She pries the box open and looks inside.

The baby is no larger than a coconut. Her tiny features twitch in her relaxed state of sleep. The baby suckles on the air around her. Tonne shuts the box. Her deepest fear is realized. She is now responsible for this creation.

Concealed within the shadows
is an imagined safety,
For the enemy hides in the darkness.

A dream, the recounting of a time when this turmoil first began, has replayed in Tonne's mind often throughout the past sixteen years. Emila is there, smiling from across a bus. She has been leading Tonne into a life of hiding, lived only to support the orchid child. Emila knows the ending to the tale. Tonne can feel what she knows but has no way to add words to her impression of anxiety.

In the dream it is quiet and the bus rides on past the inner city. The time is early in the morning. Tonne must find a place to hide before the sun becomes strong by noon. The bus comes to a stop. Emila stands and crosses the isle to Tonne's side. She removes a leather journal from her side bag, inhaling the sweet fleshy scent once more before handing it to Tonne.

Without a word, Emila disappears from the bus and into the approaching daylight. Tonne looks at the baby in one arm, asleep and precious, and then at the journal in the other. She agreed to follow Emila here. She believed it was time for some answers. Instead, Emila only added mystery to the puzzle. Tonne opens the journal and reads what is scribed on the first page.

> *Keep this soul alive. For sixteen years you must hide her in the winter's bone. Shelter her from others who will not understand. Protect her from those who wish her harm. Trust your instinct and escape if any feelings of doubt arise. Upon the morning of her sixteenth birthday, you will be released of your mission. Then you may rest.* – Emila

At the lab, Tonne signed many documents stating that she would not interfere in any way with the development of this child. She signed away her parental rights before a cell was even created. Now she is solely responsible for this being. Tonne knows that she must give her life to release her daughter. It will be done in order to fulfill the prophecy that Genue will save the world. She feels her dream disappear into the past, fading away.

Tonne awakens to the reality of dampness creeping into her broken down body and has returned from her memories to her present entrapment. Looking around, she sees only disgust. She is hidden inside a cave that is meant to conceal her existence. The morning of Genue's sixteenth birthday fills the air. Drips of molten sunlight flow into the atmosphere of the cavern. The bittersweet realization of the prophecy is set into Tonne's mind. The rest she has longed for will be her death.

Tonne attempts to move against the chains that brace her to the ground. Have they always known where she was? Did Emila set her up only to destroy her in the end? She cries at the thought of her struggle. She feels so foolish for trusting that woman, that crazy woman, so many years ago. Now, because her love is so strong for Genue, as much as she wishes to rebel her fate, Tonne gives into the sacrifice of her existence. These years have been hard, toiling and twisting her youth into the age of near death; wearing down her resilience. The rest will be welcomed after the long fight.

Tonne looks over at the form of Genue's body, chained to the ground, asleep from the bruise placed upon her cheek. She examines the room. In the center, a bucket catches water dripping from a crack in the ceiling above. She can reach it by her foot. She kicks at it with her outstretched leg and spills the collected liquid inside. The water seeps out and forms a channel, flowing toward Genue. A fine mist circles her body and is inhaled into her pores. She awakens and sees Tonne. Concern engulfs her expression as she notices the fear covering her mother's face.

> Gen, there's something I never wrote in that book. I wanted to pretend it was never there and that it never existed. Before you were created a boy was made, your brother. He has been the one hunting you and wishes you dead. Do not fall into his trap, his hate. You must defeat him with love and compassion. Do not kill him with the same heart that he will try to use and destroy you. Show him mercy but capture his soul. You must go now and leave me behind. My purpose is done. I must follow the plan of my creation. My journey has come to its climax.

> *Use your powers Genue.*
> *Whispers in her ear.*
> *Some other voice within her mind.*

The troll returns to the cavern and looks at his prize. Genue closes her eyes. She breathes deeply as her heart burns with fury. Her core begins to melt as fire escapes her form and overtakes the room. Genue emits orange and white particles of lava.

The troll turns toward her. Genue brightens and glows, pulsing the thick flame from her body. He grabs his face in agony as his skin ignites. Charred matter slides off his skeleton, flesh falling to the ground as death overcomes. The metal chains and ropes fade from Genue's wrists and ankles. She stands, pulling her energy back inside her shell, and into her molten core. Genue looks around at the destruction she has caused. Her captor is dead. Her mother is dead. She is all that remains.

-She Sleeps to Dream-

Your liquid eyes and silver tongue,
Take me where I have never been before.

Tonne is weightless as she feels the white air pressing against her figure. She takes a breath, but there is nothing to fill her lungs. In the distance she can see a sliver of pink light fill the vacant space with color, illuminating the scene around her. In front of her is a field of beautiful foliage and luscious trees. The grass is crispy under her toes.

Tonne looks around to see it all in more detail but a static interferes with the scene and as soon she can see the colors it begins to fade. The sliver of light begins to disappear and the color changes back into white. She is absorbed into the bleached nothing that is around her.

Panic sinks into her psyche. Tonne screams but no sound is released. In the distance she can hear the resonance of joyful music playing. She turns but can see only the vast sea of ivory. The static charge ripples, interrupting the void and a calm washes over her emotions. Deep within the dream, Tonne can make out the shape of a man's face. He smiles and reaches his hand toward hers. Unsure of her future, Tonne allows herself to hold him. He jerks her forward and she falls.

Tonne realizes that her eyes are squeezed shut. She can still feel the warmth of his hand in hers. She relaxes and opens her eyes. Gasp! Breath returns! Tonne looks at the kingdom in front of her. Green grass and healthy trees reach into the void. There is fruit extending from the branches! The man leads her through the jungle and to a building entrance. He smiles at her once more and presses hard against the thick wooden door. As it opens he motions her to go inside.

> Welcome home to the Inogenue. Soon you will know the secret of your life. The Oracle awaits your arrival. Don't be afraid of what is ahead of you on this journey. Time will erase your doubt.

Tonne looks back at him. She has no memory of her past. Blank. Her life is beginning. The door closes hard behind her. She walks a long hall. Paintings line the walls. She looks closely at each one, illustrating a lush green world. Further down the hall she notices that the world in the paintings become browner. Grey and mud tones are overtaking the lush green and blues. In the last painting the world is consumed with fire. The flame covering the planet begins to change into hair. It spins slowly and turns into the face of a woman. She is amazed at the sight and steps back from the imagery in front of her. The fire is her own red hair, like looking into a mirror.

> Lost in history I see. Do you like the new works? We made them for your return to us. We knew you would come back to us one day.

Tonne looks for the face to match the voice in her mind. A woman emerges from the shadows, her long ebony hair flowing to the ground. She reaches out and puts her arm around Tonne's shoulder, leading her into a room.

> The man who guided you here is your lover and wants you to not fear him. He wants you to remember him and all the things you did together. This will take time my dear. Your mind is but an infant learning to suckle. It will all come back to you.

Tonne has no memories of her life before or the life she just left behind. She doesn't remember her love for Essuel or the lives she created with her DNA. In time her memories will show themselves through her dreams. One day, all of her thoughts and experiences will rush and flood into her intellect.

The woman leads Tonne to a velvet couch and directs her to sit. She snaps her fingers in the air. A boy rushes into the room carrying a tray. On it, water and fruit, all for her. They have been awaiting her return. Tonne begins to eat the food in front of her. She isn't sure if it is hunger driving her need or just a need to fill the void. She eats it all anyway.

> I know this must seem strange to you now.
> You requested that no memories accompany
> you to Earth, as not to taint your mission. I
> am Sudne, your trusted advisor. You are of
> the Inogenue. It was your choice to save
> Earth, to plant the seed for love and hate.

Tonne stares closely at the woman standing in front of her, speaking nonsense into the air between them. She doesn't understand what she has been told. There must be some mistake. Her eyes roll into her head. Sleep is her only escape from this moment. It is all too deep.

+ + + + + + +

Genue escapes the tunnel, dragging Tonne's lifeless body behind her as she mourns her death. Now Genue must guide her own way through the existence of living. Outside, she moves rocks and logs into a circle and places her mother's corpse on top. Genue reaches into her pocket and retrieves a flint rock.

Swank!   Twinge!   POOF!

The flame is absorbed into Tonne's remains, an honorable burial, flesh returned to dust. Tears stream the tar and soot collected on Genue's cheeks. She reaches into her pocket and removes her chapstick. As she slides the moist surface across her chaffed lips, she ponders her newfound destiny. Her brother has been on this Earth as long she has. He is one like her, of their mother and of the orchid.

> The flower is slowly blossoming, peaceful. The patience of the sun is presented, marveling at the energy encompassed by chlorophyll and earth. The plant is captured and enslaved by time, caged, unable to move, alive as long as nature and man allow it. *Oh to be human*, the plant ponders, *to walk and experience life and to live among the dirt and the seas, to love beneath the stars at night.*

Genue presses her newly waxed lips together. She watches as the flame turns flesh to ash. Tonne is released and Genue must now deal with her delinquent brother. She senses that he is near. He is the poison that she has been hiding from. She wonders how far the depth of his hatred may extend.

There is a rustling behind her. Genue falls to the ground and crawls behind the flame. She begins to cry a violent outpour of emotion held within her body all these years. She releases her fear in preparation for the moment she will be discovered by the one who is hunting her.

Jubrock, drawn to the commotion ahead, follows the sounds of fire. Genue, still young and naive, does not realize the magnet she has become. All know where she is. They are tracking her scent, like oxygen to the flame, like flies to the light. He sees her lying on the ground, sobbing into her arms. The pyre embers the night sky and the darkness all around is now a blaze. Genue sits up, noticing the large figure standing in front of her.

BLANG!   CONK!   Thu-u-ud!

Genue is knocked unconscious. Quickly, Jubrock positions her body onto his stretcher, fastening her arms into a strait jacket. No man has been able to escape capture from him. He leans over her subdued body and pulls a tangle of hair from her forehead. Straw tresses of blond highlights on tarnished silver threads, glisten between the shadows of his hands.

Crimson lips of the orchid, in bloom upon her face, emit her delicate features. Her face, her lips, and her skin mesmerize Jubrock. He covers her with the burlap tarp and ties her extra tight. He will deliver his greatest bounty tonight, collect his reward, and bask in the glory of his capture of the ultimate prize, the elusive Genue. All these years she has been concealed. Sathe will be proud of him. Maybe he will be released from the monster's hold.

Jubrock smiles at his subdued prey. He turns to the front of the stretcher and begins to drag Genue across the deserted plain of land, deprived of life. The sun's prisoner is a skeleton of brambles and tumbleweeds that shrink below her reach.

-His Descent Below-

Sathe, we lay in the
Streets by the bay,
lost amongst the piles of decay.

The boys of pre-pubescence chant their song together, taunting the monster to stir within. They always sing the same salute of stupidity. The boys crowd together as there is more power with more than one. They struggle to claim the gold metal, to be the superior leader of their ruffian pack, like a pride of cubs striving to become the alpha male.

Sathe stands, holding his ground, standing firmly all the days of his ten years on this Earth. Unfortunately, he falls all the way down, turning away from the pressures of forgiveness, and giving into the welcoming arms of revenge. He wants a new life, the cost is of no matter, for her soul he will trade. He lies. He steals. He cheats. He does whatever it takes to stay one step ahead. Always out for number one: Sathe.

The wall, I have built so tall.
My hatred, the mortar.
My resentment, building the bricks,
Piece by solid piece.
To hide in front of the world.
Impossible, but I do it everyday.

These boys singing that stupid song in my face do not know what they do. I think, as they laugh their stupid laugh, of how many ways I can stop their hearts with just my fingertips. I plan my ultimate victory as they bask in the glory of their immediate gratification.

I can touch them with poison fingers. I did that before. It happened the first time at a sleepover with some neighborhood kids. We were all nano-kids, or so they thought. It was ruled out an unexplained heart attack. We friends crowded and sobbed the loss of our companion. He was an annoying little brat. Someone was going to off him eventually. I figure I did society a service. Poison touches. Anyone who gets close to me dies. When I excite I become toxic. When I anger, I become lethal. To anyone who stirs my curiosity…I kill.

My mother is a scientist and a doctor. She tries to "figure me out" and find out "what's wrong now". She is always running tests on me, trying to "fix" me. It is misery. Just leave me alone to be the killer I was born to be. She often disappears into her laboratory to write notes in that stupid leather book as she files samples of my green blood away for later use.

Mother dyes my hair like the chestnut shade of the nano children. This is done so I can blend into society as one of them. After only a few days, it has already faded with an auburn sunburst illuminating from underneath, beneath the shadows of the disguise. My joy is washed away by the tears of her desperation, her only wish being to make me more human.

My mother needs a redhead woman to complete her study. Somehow this is the answer to my salvation. The girls show up at my house. I watch them behind my door, through the crack right before it is shut. Our house is comparable to a sorority with women everywhere, but none of them have a red hair on their head. My mother, always willing to try, returns to the room informing whatever girl who's DNA she has just denied, that her services will not be needed. Out with her, in with more. There is always a new girl to replace the other.

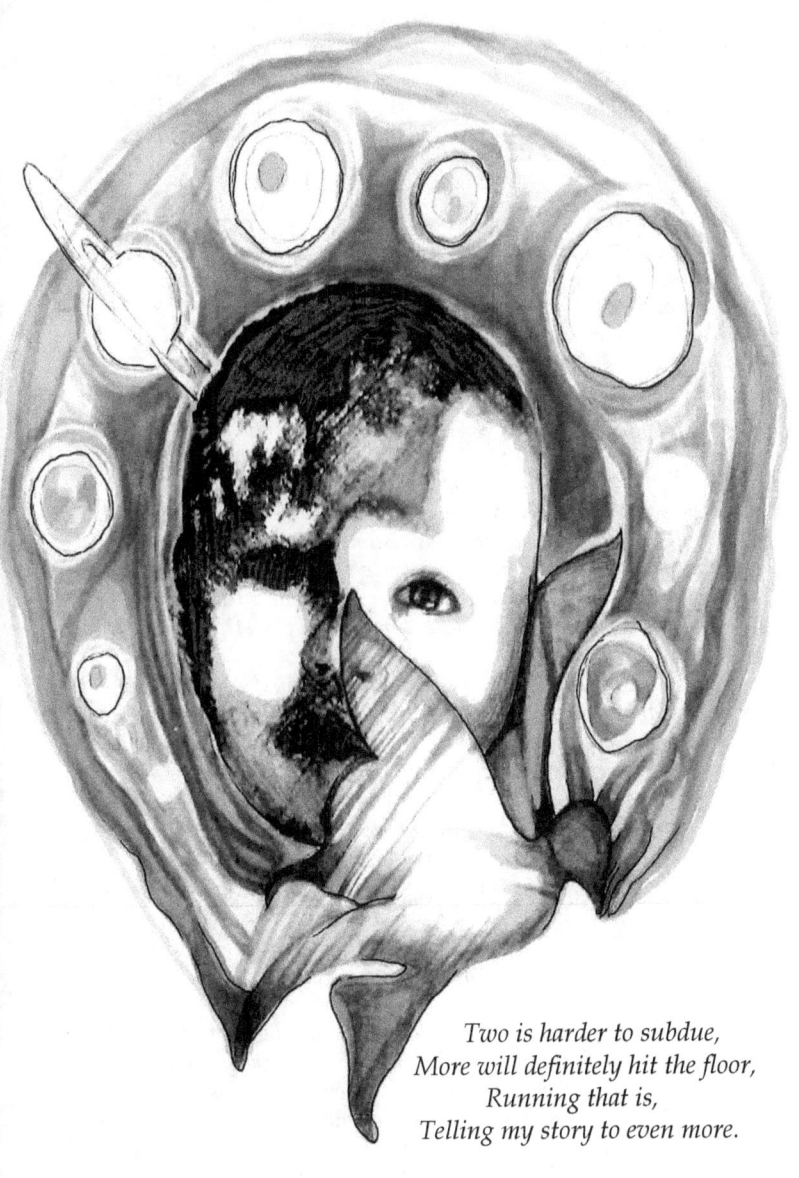

Two is harder to subdue,
More will definitely hit the floor,
Running that is,
Telling my story to even more.

Luxury. My mother's career affords us much of the finer things in life. Our mansion, inhabited only by her and myself, sits right outside of town, overlooking our peasants like a queen perched on her throne. Mother's disfigured legs barely carry her the many steps her days require. She was burned in some fire…so she says…she barely escaped with her life. Pity her. Evil woman.

Orchids are everywhere, adorning any surface of our home that can be covered, growing in twists, reaching for the skylight cut into the roof. She makes me hide in this dungeon, away from the sun, away from the women and her.

Mother knows the real story behind Nanotechnology. She is the leading technician in Nano-tech research. She fights the reopening of the Biolarity Lab, explaining that nano-robots are computers used to heal, whereas Biolarity uses human life to cure people. It's a trade of longer life for one's soul and the possibility of living forever. The other promises that youth will remain just a while longer knowing one day you will malfunction and die. Her testimony sounds good, I suppose, except that she comes to me and extracts my green magic. It is used to rejuvenate her sun-damaged flesh. Hypocrite. Cheating death. Survival. For what, another day on this twisted planet?

Freezing cold seeps into my mind. I am reminded of my current reality. My attention is returned to the boys I must refrain from murdering. The one kid, who taunts my patience, now stands in front of mine. He has my attention.

Sathe I lay
in the street myself,
holding his face
that I beat,
trying hard
not to slay.

I remember now where my life is standing still. I think of the countless ways I can kill this imbecile. I laugh at his new song, more original than the others I have heard. I feel my poison grow as my laughter ignites. I reach toward his face, threatening me. I can't, not now. There are too many of them. But oh how I would love to grab him, just for a moment, and welcome my satisfaction as poison seeps from my fingers into his meat, my glory.

Instead, I reach into my pocket. I feel for my rock. The heat from my own hand burns into the smooth surface. I bring my accomplice from seclusion and introduce it into the situation. I launch it with all my stored force within. Contact! His motive has changed to cowardice, as I have taken his bluff and thrown it away.

Blood, beautiful blood, sprays my entire being. I lick my lips and taste the iron that I myself am lacking. I hear his screams, music to my ears. It is quite a sight to see. The other boys run to safety, leaving this one in my company, all alone. I lean forward equal to his face, mouth and teeth mangled from the blow of the stone. I continue forward and pick up my rock. As I stand I can't help myself and I touch the cut on his lip with my poison finger. I connect my energy to his flesh and at once the destruction is set into motion. Green travels through his membranes. I stand back as he wilts to the ground, now a useless heap of flesh and bone.

I am taken away, chained and caged like the animal I want to be. I will forever spend my days in the asylum. At age ten, disgraced. I live as a crazy person, exiled from my home and my mother. Alone. Forgotten. She gave me over to them. Insane. Imperfect. They are afraid of what I am. The others who inhabit this asylum of defunct disease and tortuous thoughts are nothing like me. I sit alone.

Days pass with just my insanity and my torturous thoughts trapped together inside my head. I begin to imagine my life as it has come to be. Then the unimaginable happens. She comes to see me. I can't believe she is standing there looking at me. I want to hide in the white linens that I sit upon. I want to grow into the wooden frame that supports my bed. My mother, Emila, the traitor, has presented herself into my company. She motions to the guards to leave us alone. I lick my teeth as I smile at them, a habit I have grown to rather enjoy. I decide that I will not be speaking to her.

> I know that you will not be speaking to me,
> Sathe, but this is best. There is no place for
> you in society. I will still remain your doctor
> and will be visiting you weekly to analyze
> your fluids. I want you to know the truth.

I watch her as she takes out the leather bound book from her bag. The book that is my history, the one I have been watching her add to all these years. She has chronicled my life on the pages, detailing the timeline of my existence.

This is my journal. No one else can see this or they will kill you. I wrote this for you in case this day ever came, a day when solitude is best. I knew this day would come and I am sorry for the result.

She reaches out to me and places the book at the end of my bed. A peace offering I suppose. I watch her standing there, hovering like a vulture over a decaying carcass. Controlling my life. Writing my story. Was this a chapter in her book? So much to handle, I'll just put him away. I feel my disgust for her grow. Passion is seeping through my veins, flowing out of my mouth with each labored breath I take. It consumes every shred of my being. I break my vow of silence.

Do I frighten you that much? Are you afraid that I might do it to you? I could graze you with my poison touch. Is this why you hide me away in this prison to rot while you live on experiencing life? It is because you know I hold your life in my hands. Without me you would crumble to dust. I guess you never thought I would figure out my place in your life....my place of importance.

Her blank stare reassures me that I have struck a chord, deep inside her, so I continue my speech. I want to make her crumble. I want to take what is left of her dignity and destroy it.

Then why, if such concern for your own life did you have the guards leave? They were your only salvation. Now, I am the holder of your fate. I have already killed you. Don't you feel the emptiness of my stare? I too have grown in power.

By this time she is so entranced by my seeping chlorophyll, she doesn't notice that I have become merely inches from her face. I smile at her, looking one last time at her aged skin that once dressed in youth. She has been off of my serum for too long. It shows. I lean forward and lick her pasty, sun washed flesh, her cheek. Protruding eyes scream in pain as she falls to the floor. Her body jerks and seizes uncontrollably. A fighter. She must know her battle has already been lost.

Someone! Anyone, take her away!

The guards run in but it is too late. She is gone. I sit back on my bed and lean against the cold cinderblock wall. I squeeze the leather book in my hand. Remembering there are secrets that lie within, I tuck it into the back of my pants as I watch the spectacle play out in front of me. I smile at the guards and allow a slight chuckle to escape as I watch them scramble to collect the crime scene of my life. She had it coming, her death. It was her fault. She had protection but chose not to use it. What an ego. I am ready for them to get out so I can begin my novel, thanks to ole mom.

‑Camp of Detachment‑

Solid dirt supports the flesh,
Nourishing the growth all around.

Silence creeps in between the creases of the stillness surrounding the two boys. A night of adventure, Essuel and Annuil camp below the vast night sky. Their father has brought them to Earth. It is now their home. He watches above hovering over the boys like a vulture preparing to feast.

> Annuil, don't you ever wish we were free to make our own life, one not controlled by father and his wishes? I just want to make my own way and meet people of all kinds and fall in love with whoever I want.

> All I want is to make father proud. He expects much of me and I cannot disappoint him, Essuel.

> Or what! Or he will give the throne to me, his rightful heir!

I never said that! I am the legitimate heir! You cannot deny me that right. I never chose to be created but now that I am I will carry my duty with honor and destroy all that aim to mangle my path. Even you brother, will never take that from me.

Essuel imagines killing him now. He imagines tearing the beating heart from his torso and throwing it into the abyss. He sees the coward for what he is, a slave to his father's demands.

Annuil, you are no brother to me. My brother, the one who I agreed to come to this planet and complete this mission with, has been replaced with a brainwashed fool! You can have our father. I don't need either of you, but I promise you this, I will return and I will remove you from my kingdom!

Essuel escapes the camp and walks toward the rising sun. He will do the mission alone and plans to show his father what a failure Annuil is. He cannot survive without Essuel's backbone and will eventually crumble.

I will tell father that you have left! I will tell him that you denounced his power to me! Essuel, you will die out there in the wilderness!

Screams from Annuil follow behind his steps. Nothing could change Essuel's mind now. He imagines his father's disappointment when he returns to find that Annuil has recoiled and cried like a baby. Essuel decides he will build a water source for the humans. Hydraulic energy. His father will be so proud of him.

Essuel daydreams of his mother while he walks through the jungle of bramble weeds. In his dreams he can see her skin, iridescent turquoise flesh, beauty that no one can comprehend. The precious son would stare at his mother all day. He would slide his cherub fingers across her arm and watch the dazzling colors sparkle in his energy.

*I will be with you forever. I will even bring my
bride to live alongside you, my mother. I will
always love you, forever my sweet dragon lady. I
will never betray you.*

*I know my boy. I will always be with you, even
when you can't see me.*

The mother smiles at her young son's virtuous declarations. She
can't mutter the words of truth that she will not live another
day. She will not tell her young boy that he will be taken away
with his father to save him from the tyrannical lizard king. She
was to marry him but will be killed instead for loving Essuel's
father. She must accept her fate. She will keep her pain inside.
The dragon leans over and kisses her offspring once more
before he is taken away. That is as far as his memories will take
him to wander.

That was the last time Essuel saw his mother. He can see her in
his dreams when they meet in the collected consciousness. He
calls to her for answers. He feels her guiding him down his path
of fate. She will lead him to the waters edge and he will make
hydraulics. His father will be impressed.

Many days pass without any interaction between the boys.
Essuel works the trench by the beach to lead the water through
his garden. He constructs a small cabin in the trees to protect
him from the elements. In the distance he hears a rustle in the
woods. Essuel looks out from his shelter and stares into the
tangle of vines and overgrown vegetation.

Essuel! Essuel, show your face to me now boy! I
can feel that you are near and I did not raise you
as a coward!

It is his father, returned to see the progress his sons have made
to tame the wilderness on their own. The young boy takes a
deep breath and walks out to speak with his origin.

I am here. I have looked forward to seeing you
again and showing you what I have…

Stop now, Essuel. I care not what you have done on your own here. The whole purpose of this mission was for you and your brother to work in harmony and lead your workers. I fear not the working you have succeeded on your own, but that you left Annuil to die!

To die! Please father, do spare me the dramatics of this incident. If he wishes to die then let him do so. I will fight for my day here on this Earth. I have irrigated the water here to my camp and I have confirmed my leadership while he has proven his weakness. He will never make a fearless king and will hand over the crown you worked so hard to preserve, to a stronger tribe. He has validated his lack of worth.

Essuel, I never put a soldier expectation on your brother. I have always known he is physically weak. I am aware that you are strong my son. What I fear is that your strength will lead to tyranny if you are allowed. I am not denying your dragon heritage my boy. You are the most powerful of my sons. You got your power from your mother.

She sacrificed her life for you father! They killed her because of you! You didn't even fight for her honor. You let them tear the heart from her flesh. How could you father? She was to be a queen!

The old king sits on a log rotting into the ground. He places his hands on his knees to brace himself. The father's anger is replaced with sadness as he recounts a time with the boy's mother. He thinks of her sparking skin as he touches her shoulder in his mind.

The boy will never understand the politics of marriage. Unions within the family of the universe are planned upon birth. She was to be wed to the great lizard king and as much as their love could endure, they would never overthrow the decision to kill her. It was her *penance*. She thrust the boy into his arms and begged him to flee with the child to safety or they would both be destroyed forever.

> The anger dripping from your poisonous words will never allow the forgiveness necessary to understand why we left. The throne cannot be yours because of this. You will not rule the people here, infecting them with your cancer of rage. It will be Annuil.

The father rises and leaves Essuel alone with the depth of his thoughts. The boy watches as he leaves. The displeasure of his situation teases his intellect, twisting his psyche into a knot of resentment and outrage. The old king doesn't know of the things the dragon queen taught her son. He isn't aware that Essuel knows how to create life from the king's precious starseeds. The slow burn of Essuel's idea begins to form. He will create his own people and they will defeat Annuil's race. They will feel the love and hate, a gift from the Inogenue. He signs his plan with sparrow's blood and stores it deep within the ventricles of his heart.

-THE BLOODY CHILD-

Led by arm into the darkness,
Upon the light of the moon, they run.
Among the shadows and below the naked trees,
By the cloak of night, they run.

GENUE!

She hears her name spoken. Pre-pubescent games of hormonal angst drift between the children in the hall. Genue stops walking. She is holding her dolls arm, stroking the top of each knobby finger with her thumb. The arm is all that remains after her doll was sacrificed to the flame for her survival. The porcelain is cold in her hand. She rubs the fine porous clay, imagining that it is bone, an extension of her own self.

Genue is a child of nine at this time. She is old enough to realize that she has the power and control over what kind of person she will become. She exudes the confidence of a lion, hanging on to her pride like a golden ticket. She will give no reply to her name.

Genue, you're a Brat!

The threat is coming from Leerah, her adversary and her greatest challenge. There a battle between the two girls, begun by jealousy and maintained by the covetous fuel of hatred. Leerah waits for her spark to set fire. She wants Genue to fall apart.

I know what you are!

Leerah smirks and nods to the three other girls standing with her. They all know Genue is different. On the outside she could pass for containing nanotechnology, although, she does not. She is more than the machines could ever be. When sunlight touches her skin, a static charge occurs generating a ripple along her proportions. She recharges, far superior to that of the nano-people.

Genue must hide her abilities from those like Leerah, who could never understand the world beyond what is merely presented on the outside. Misunderstood by those with eyes closed to anything that may cause the discomfort of change.

+ + + + + + +

The Sun: Enemy Number One.

Theories circulate of what caused the sun to expand. The phenomenon happened instantly. Some speculate that a meteor was engulfed into the massive fire, adding mass to the core. Others claim a covert government mission disposed of nuclear waste and weaponry from Earth. Then there are those people who have theorized, researched, and explained the occurrence to that of nature running its own evolutionary course through time; explaining that the sun itself has matured into a new phase of development. The effect on Earth and its inhabitants has been devastating. They will never know the truth.

An alter-life exists after the sun rests. Most people that remain cannot afford a procedure such as Nanotechnology for sun protection. The affluent and those able to upgrade look in disgust at the others, the less fortunate. Those unable to attain such scientific measures for survival are forced into subways and into the underworld. The humans who survived the solar apocalypse, retreat in caverns under the surface, into the forgotten bellows of society.

Nano-cells, powered by sunlight, receive a charge from the magisterial rays pouring onto earth. Throughout the day the upgraded body is restored. The brain of one with Nanotechnology, retains all memories, filing knowledge and information into organized compartments of the mind. The advanced human operates at the optimal performance rate. The contemporary life of Earth appears to be that of a fairytale. The Singularity is here. The zombie nation will be born from this new reality.

The upgraded humans build beautiful schools and mansions across the vacant land. Empty bodies are burned and entire cities are pulverized, making way for the alterations of life. Machines cover the rubble with new earth, burying the past below. The machines construct spectacular buildings of glass to marvel and view the astounding womb of land around them.

+ + + + + + +

Genue is alone with her exceptionality, inside the confines of her secret room. She crawls up the ladder at midday, when the others in the colony are asleep. She steps into the room of windows and looks out across the sea of Earthly fire. A city, smoldering, with its inhabitants forced to retreat underground, is all that remains.

Genue often slips away into her fortress of windows to watch the offspring of the upgraded humans playing in the courtyard that lies just beyond the borders of her refuge. She watches them dance in the sunlight. Their silky tresses keeping beat, flirting with the passing breeze, as they play in the outside. She is drawn into their activity. She longs to see more.

> One leg out the window. Hold on tight.
> The other leg, torso, head.
> Freedom. Uncontained curiosity gives way.

Genue runs along the parameter of the yard, the only safety to the underground refuge. She pauses to see if anyone has noticed her presence, then crawls to the gate. Upon closer inspection she notices that the children all have the same color of hair, the hue of rich dark chocolate syrup.

Genue takes her notebook from her back pocket and sketches the figure of one of the children. She adds the blue pinstripe pants that the boys are wearing. To the side she jots down a simple jumper to illustrate what the girls are wearing. She is ignorant to the interest of one of her subjects.

What's your name?

Startled, Genue falls back onto the balls of her hands, feeling the snap of her pencil breaking beneath her fingers. She drops her sketch on the ground behind her back, taking in the sight of the most beautiful girl she has ever seen. The children from the underworld are ashen mud from the dirt that surrounds them. Genue's own strands of gold appear tarnished and dingy. The girl standing in front of her has long clean hair, sparkling and reflecting the bright sun. She notices an amber aura of energy swarming the girl's petite frame.

Genue's breath escapes the safety of her lips and anxiety creeps in from the corners of her mind. All she knows is to escape. She gathers her things and runs back to her sanctuary. What would come of this meeting? Would the girl tell anyone she was there? She rests her body against the wall of her fortress and looks back across the valley, exchanging stares with the robot children. Genue watches them as they turn back to their game and ease themselves once more into the comfort of play.

The offspring, born unto parents who are genetically altered by Nanotechnology, are mutant. This outcome was not predicted. Each new birth results in the same skin, hair, and eyes. The same look and expressions come from each tiny face.

Puzzled by the duplicated occurrence, doctors and scientists enroll the pint-sized patients into their studies. The offspring are found to naturally build immunity against the growing sun. Their creamy complexion never tans nor burns. The head is adorned with chestnut tresses that never fade. Complete with hazel eyes that never flicker in pain. It is determined that these mutations are actually a positive transformation in the human genetic gene pool.

At birth, tattoos are etched onto the bottom of each baby's right foot. The last name of the family, followed by the number of birth order, distinguishes the flesh. This is the only reminder of ancestry and traits that are lost in the machine's lineage. The shared identity is the new uniform placed on the product of the altered reproduction cycle. A new supercomputer is created out of the ignorance of the people as one by one they offer up their precious soul to live forever. The endless capabilities encourage the countless possibilities to live in harmony with the exploding star. Science has won, for now.

Genue climbs through the window, back into the room, and rolls over into the corner. She looks at her arm glowing radiant aqua hues that are seeping from her entire body. Her only mission is to retreat back into the colony. She leaves to find her mother. As she walks the length of the corridor back to her home she can feel her nemesis staring into her back.

> Gen, why is your body blue?

Leerah has been waiting for her return. Startled, Genue looks down at her body emitting a sea of swirling blue energy, alternating shades of turquoise and sapphire.

> What is wrong with you?

Frightened by the scene, Leerah begins to scream. Genue escapes and runs to her home. Tonne is waiting for her to return. She pushes the door open as her mother releases the lock.

> Mother, you won't believe what happened to me!

By this time the indigo aura has been replaced with the constant gold hues that normally evaporate from her skin. She catches her breath in the excitement of her situation. Genue continues:

> I went outside and I saw a girl, an upgrade
> offspring, and when I returned my skin was
> BLUE! What is that?

Tonne gasps, covering her mouth to hide her fears. She steps toward Genue and reaches her hand to grasp her daughter's wrist. She can still see a light sea flicker from the surface of her skin.

> You what!?! Do you know how dangerous that was?

BANG! BANG! KNOCK!

Tonne looks out the eyehole of the door. Standing on the other side is Leerah and an official guard of the colony. She turns back to Genue and motions her go into the bedroom. She makes a hand signal for sleep. Tonne takes in a deep breath and opens the door. She stares at her unwelcome visitors. No words pass the neutral zone between them. Through the silence she searches for a greeting.

> Yes, is there something I can help you with?

Leerah stares at Tonne with the challenge of retreat smeared into the smirk on her face. Genue listens to the voices in the main room. She can smell the fear and taste the excitement in the air. She expects to hear answers, always knowing that her reality is different than that of others. She hears the voices getting closer. Tonne speaks to her daughter in the other room.

> Gen, are you asleep? Leerah has come by to see you. I don't mean to wake you. Would you like to visit with her?

Genue sits up in the bed. Blink – Blink – Blink. Make it look real; she thinks to herself, looking over at Leerah, she coils a grin with her mouth.

> Genue! You were in the hall, in that room, and you were blue! Your skin was a glowing fog!

Leerah, confused and disbelieving, turns to her officer. He scowls at her and walks back toward the door, annoyed with the wasted time spent in the politics of children.

> Where are you going? Oh Leerah, you must not
> have found what you were looking for.

Genue laughs into the tension of the situation as she lays back down, smiling at her victory. Under the covers she listens as the voices become softer. Door open. Door shut. Tonne runs back into the room where Genue is laying down.

> We are leaving NOW!

Genue knew this day would come. There is no room for discussion or argument. She has no choice but to follow her mother into the wilderness of the wandering nothing. They are nomads, homeless on this mainland of misery, forever searching for the promise of anything.

> Did you even get water while you were out
> making a scene?

They both know the answer. Genue looks down at her feet, greyed from the earth outside. She shakes her head. No. She will have to go back out. Only the children of the colony are permitted into the walls of the water well. In order to prevent excessive use, they carry as much water as a body of their size can hold, each day, to their family. Tonne would not survive the travel without water. No words pass between mother and daughter. Genue stands from her chair and walks to the door, grabbing two empty jugs to carry with her.

> Hey, be careful. Meet me at the edge and don't
> talk to anyone.

Genue exits the pod. She already feels Leerah's revenge. The hallway is clear of people for now. A flow of an oleaginous substance winds its way down the center of the narrow walkway. Genue is glad to escape this hole, the cluster-phobic bowl of misery. At the entrance of the well, two boys look at cards together. She walks by, uninterested in child's play.

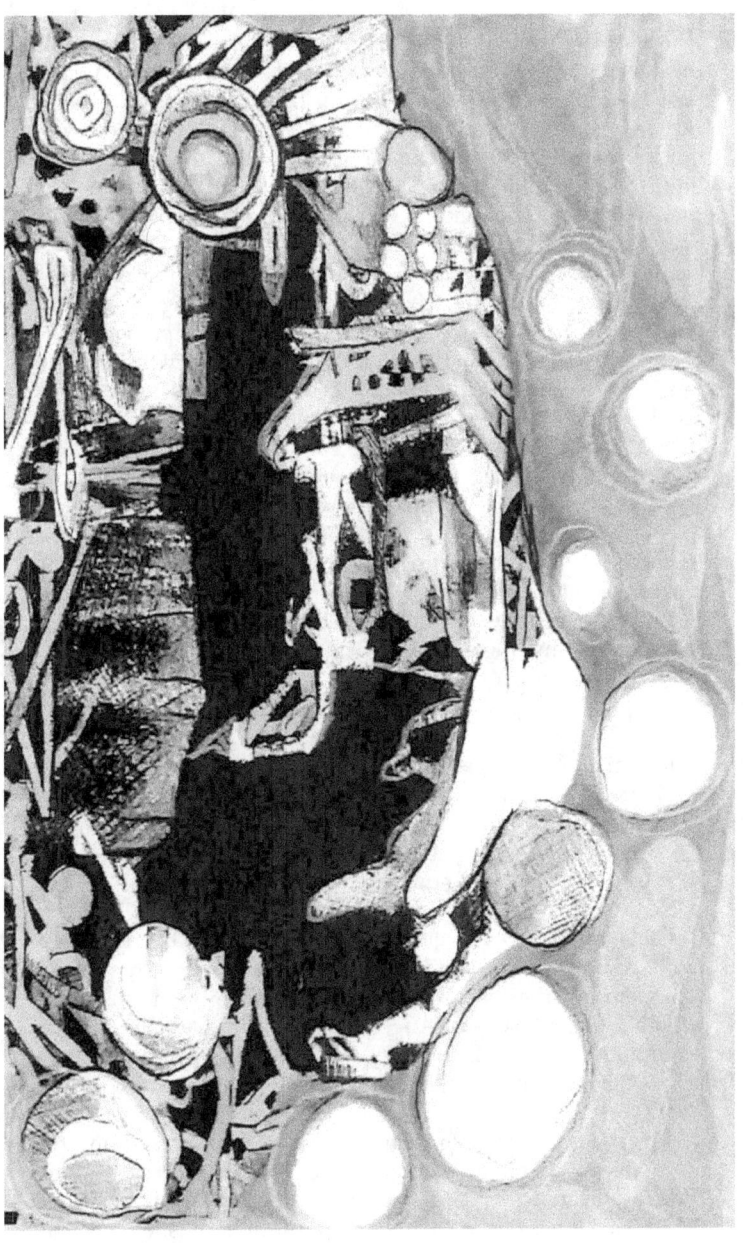

Ahead is the well. Holding her jug under the spout, she pulls the lever out, and releases the molecules of life. They gently pass in front of her eyes. A light mist floats outward from the rim and toward her awaiting pores. Genue is thirsty, however, quickly satisfied by the escaping fog, as the tiny particles of liquid seep into her skin. Now jug 2. Done. She begins the return to meet her mother. It will be night soon.

Genue walks slowly and carefully avoiding all the eyes that look at her. She can feel Leerah's revenge getting closer. The dinner hall is all that stands in the way of her completion of the mission. Girls gather in the kitchen, discussing in whispers and muted giggles. She picks up her speed. Her shoes screech across the damp floor, alerting everyone to her presence.

> Look ladies, it's the chameleon. Are you
> going to blend into the wall to?

It is in fact Leerah leading the investigation. Genue calmly places the jugs of life at her feet. She reaches into her pocket and feels for her treasure. It is in her hand before realizing that she is stroking the tiny fingers.

> Genue. You're a brat!

Genue grips the porcelain tight in her hand. She must defend her honor. Her pride. No response, only the dagger sharp edge of silence.

> I know what you are!

Genue's mind races over the possibilities that Leerah could likely connect in her mind and think to know about her. Eager to experience the entertainment, the other children encourage Leerah to move in closer. Anger explodes within as Genue spins around on the balls of her feet. At once, she throws the doll arm across the room and into Leerah's unsuspecting face!

The eye erupts, spraying crimson, blood escaping, staining the air between them. Leerah grabs her face in horror as pain radiates through her body and she falls to her knees. Genue comes back to reality, realizing the physical harm she has done. Grabbing the jugs, she exits, running to meet Tonne.

Genue cries into the rings of hair stuck to her skin by sweat and blood. Agony. Guilt. Resentment. How could she loose control? How could she hurt another? She has never caused pain to someone else. She has never released blood before this moment. Genue does not bleed. Her cells repair themselves before fluids can escape. The beauty of her plasma is alive and delicious. Genue sees her mother. She runs into Tonne's arms.

I made this all worse, mother! Everywhere was Leerah's blood!

Tonne pulls Genue from her and looks into her eyes. She sees the war within her daughter. It wouldn't be long. Time with her child is running short. She must give her up soon. Tonne can feel them watching her and finding entertainment in how this will all play out. She wonders if they are controlling Genue and if the pain inflicted has been guided by their wishes. Home will never contain them again. A new life must begin, far from this wasteland, the trap of existence.

-History Tells the Way-

Ahead is the most unknown,
Wilderness of the barren land.

Essuel's cavern is hidden within the Syrian desert of the Middle Eastern territory of the world. It is a paradise concealed by the dry agony of the pounding sun. Annuil would never think to look past the mirage of sand to see the lush green foliage growing around the cave entrance. Essuel has tucked his secrets away where he assumes none will venture. He leads his bride across the threshold of his home.

They walk together, into the dimly lit entrance of the cave. Essuel cups his hands around his lips and blows his breath of fire into the listless air. Light grows from the nothing and sight is restored. Walls of painted imagery dance to the tale of mystery. The story laid out before her is of anguish and defeat, where many lost their lives. A story is told of love that was lost. There is a somber feeling radiating from the corners of the enclosure.

Toiling and twisting in the embers of our circumstance.

Tonne, this is the history of the Inogenue. Up there in the corner is my true mother. She was a queen of the dragons. She would have ruled the cosmos of our universe, however, she was sacrificed so that I may live. She taught me what I am about to show you. Only a dragon can harness energy. Since I am only half dragon, I need the fire of a redheaded goddess. You are the missing piece.

Essuel, I am trying to understand what you want of me. Are we going to make humans of flesh and blood? Does your father know about this project?

He will not find out until it is too late. A single ant can be killed easily by stepping on it with your foot or mashing it between your fingers. However, an army of ants is much harder to combat. In large numbers, the poison in the bite from the unified ants can destroy the strongest of an opponent. I want to give them the passion of love. I want to take from my father what he took from me! My mother had the purity of emotion and gave me the instruction I need to rule this lifetime. I am ready to create my army of ants. I must overthrow him before he passes the throne to my brother.

Tonne has no words in response. She looks closely at the murals and tries to piece the story together. Dragons scatter the walls in various stages of death and defeat. Large men of golden hues fire arrows and daggers into the sides of the enormous reptiles. Swirls of blue cyclone in and around the figures. A world explodes in the distance.

Tonne walks closer to it for a clear understanding. Red engulfs the entire panel. From the fire can be seen a small aircraft flying to a remote golden orb. She looks back to Essuel for an explanation.

That is my father's Venus and it is where he took me to live my days as a young boy. It is also the place where he replaced my mother and me with his wife and legitimate heir, Annuil. There is the seed of Earth. Isn't she beautiful?

Yes she is. I am amazed that she started out so small. A tiny seed.

We must finish the story. We must create life here worth living. Annuil and his drones are sickening. They have no soul, no feelings of joy. We must change that. Only through the tug of emotion will we ever have a spiritual being strong enough to fight for our freedom from my father.

Show me how we will do it, Essuel. You know that I love you and will help you in all that you need. Please assure me that you feel the same for me.

Essuel leans close to her face. He can smell the sweet jasmine within her aura. He kisses her softly on the forehead and slides his arms around her shoulders. Tonne breathes in his aroma of sweat and sandalwood. She loves him with her life. She will follow him to her death and he knows this.

Essuel takes Tonne's hand and leads her to the center of the room. The particles of floating light circle and weave around her glowing red strands. Together they sit on the cold dusty floor. She looks deep into his eyes for explanation but he reveals nothing. He begins to stir the soil with one hand as he pulses the air with his other. The particles are drawn into his aura. He points at the incent spheres floating in the arid depth surrounding them.

These are starseeds. They are the building blocks of the soul. The only way to animate the physical avatar of life is to tie a starseed into its center. This will create the heart, the factory of vitality.

Essuel reaches his hand toward her unruly hair and strokes it with his outstretched fingers. Swiftly, he plucks a strand free. Tonne grabs her scalp and questions his sudden action with her eyes.

> There must be a catalyst. We must tie the beat of the seeds together. The fire from your strand of hair will draw the seeds in and trap them inside a heartbeat that I will create from the nothing.

Essuel stops stirring the dirt and places one end of her hair into the center and encourages the strand to suspend vertically in the air. The starseeds are entranced by the glistening molten red color. They attach themselves along the length of her tress of glistening fire.

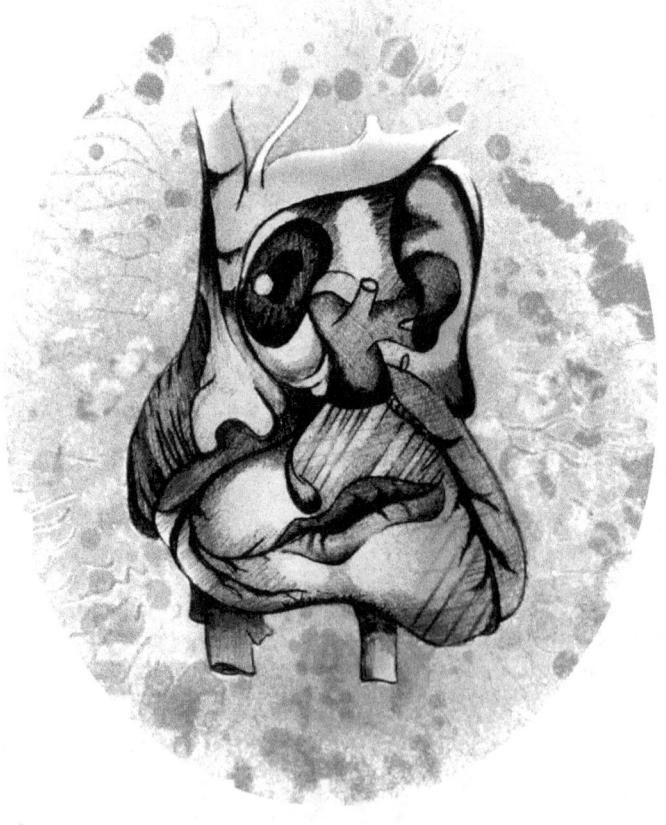

Essuel circles his hands around the seeds as they turn the strand into a helix. The spiral gets larger and a cylinder is formed. He reaches inside and grabs the end of the hair and pulls it through the center. Pulsing bright light takes over the room. Tonne screams as her eyes are forced shut by the glare. Essuel pumps the dirt, knots the fiber, and forms the heart of what will be a human.

> Tonne! Look what we have made! It is a heart! The soul will live in here. We have accomplished what my brother cannot! We have made life with the capacity to love and hate.

> Essuel, is this a good thing to do? Do you think this will become more than we can handle one day? What are we to do when your father hears of this or sees it for himself? He is a beast and I fear the torture he will rain on us for this power you have shared with me.

> Tonne! Never be afraid! Fear is what has kept you and I trapped under his control. Don't you want to be free? Don't you want to rule our planet without his condescending presence? We must build our nation. My mother gave me this knowledge for this purpose. She will guide our mission and protect us.

Tonne takes a deep breath. Her world will never be the same. She will forever be an outcast now. Her love of Essuel will lead her down a dark and lonely path. She stands from the ground and walks out of the room. The blaring sun tans her forehead. This planet will forever be her home now, her mother ship that she will never depart.

-She Stirs the Pot-

Life is conceived.
With her hands she creates a seed,
The fire of vitality.

Genue is an awkward balance of purity and truth at the young age of thirteen. She soaks the world into her pores. She drinks from the air all negative vibes and in turn excretes compassion and love. Genue is beauty, serenity, and peace, but she is misunderstood by all the pubescent numbskulls she must blend in with.

> Just give them a chance, Gen. They are only children like you. They do not understand you and must be shown who you are.

Tonne always pushes her daughter to give the other children an opportunity to prove themselves to her as harmless. Her shy, outcast appeal keeps her mother concerned of her standing out and being noticed. Genue escapes into the outdoors at midday while the others are sleeping. The heat drains the energy of Earth, even below the surface, and its inhabitants must preserve their spirit through sleep.

The people of the Earth, untouched by the Singularity epidemic, hibernate, while the nanos walk the surface, living by day and sleepless by night. Genue can do both. She could live above the surface if her fate were different. Maybe, if someone different raised her, someone above the surface, she could pass as a nano. On some days her skin seems to crawl. She is anxious with the desire to venture into her element, the sun, her nourishment. Tonne knows this and allows this, but only for her daughter's survival. Genue needs the sunlight.

On this day, Genue escapes to the surface, careful not to alarm anyone. She runs to her dirt pile beneath an abandoned pagoda on the beach. It was once a resting place for travelers to sit and collect thoughts. Now it is a refuse, a lonely reminder of the rubble that remains from the pleasures of the past. She sits atop the pile of dirt and sediment.

Genue's oily pre-teenage skin glistens in the egregious sun. She strokes the soft granules of sand with her hands. Warm pebbles ricochet from finger to finger. She scoops the powder into her palms and the grains slip and spray to the ground. Moving to a squat, she rests her head on her folded knee. Daydreams stumble inside her mind. Thoughts wander through her intellect.

What am I?
How can I go outside and live among the sun,
while others cannot?

Genue stirs the sand with vigor as the frustration cycles and grows through her particles. Charge. Electricity. The spark of life begins to emerge beneath her hands. Orange. Yellow. Pink. Genue watches in amazement at the magic taking place in front of her. With her inner instinct, she leans over the edge of her swirling storm and spits her magic into the center of the tornado. Turquoise flashes and sweeps into the scene, leaving a mark on the soil. She feels the life traveling from her fingertips into the earth. A budding vine of a plant forms.

Genue hovers over her sprouted vine, balancing gracefully on her knees. She grabs a handful of sand and releases the blessing onto her creation. Where desolate nothingness once was, now life begins. She thrusts her hands into the cool topsoil and pulses her fingers under the tiny plant, encouraging it to increase. A green vine winds out from the earth. Leaves unfold and the bud emerges.

Genue lies back to recharge. She watches her offspring thrive and grow as she feels her own pubescence develop, her body longs to be one with the sands of the Earth. She looks at her hands of a creator. She is at once amazed with her dormant powers awakening to their ultimate mission. The silence is shaken.

Genue is distracted by a figure moving in the field behind her. She crawls under a bench in hopes of blending in with the depressing surroundings. By this time the zombie nation is born. Without a successful alternative created, people continue to accept the Singularity as the only answer.

The people who allow the robots into their body systematically loose touch with the reality of the world around them. Desiring more youth, longing to feel more alive, these prisoners of the new society search endlessly for something to fill the void. Glitches and viruses infect those unable to maintain their changed physical composition; slowly withering away, becoming the outcasts they so desperately tried to avoid.

One doctor theorized that if a person suffering from this robot affliction ingests pure, unaltered human flesh, all of the distorted particles would be excreted and replaced with healthy cells. As awful as this may sound, the degenerate brains of these monsters accept this proposal.

Underground caverns have been ambushed. The humans discovered living within are captured and caged like animals. They are to be brought into the laboratories to test the new theory, if they aren't eaten first by their captors. When the humans learn that their own life matter is prey to the evil machine, they absorb the reality that it is the end of peace. The war has begun.

Word spreads quickly of these new practices. The humans devise procedures to protect their virgin flesh. Entrances to the camps are fortified. Committees are elected to organize the resistance. If out of grounds travel is necessary, mud and other decayed matter will be applied to the skin. This sludge disguises the delicious aroma of pure human elements. A new fear has risen from the chaos of this unknown life of survival. Now the humans must hide from the starving nano-zombies in order to avoid consumption.

Genue watches as a woman walks into her view. The woman is tired and decrepit. Her tattered dress sways with each sauntering step. This creature will hunt Genue like an animal. The tower is only about one hundred feet away. Genue could run the distance and reach the ladder. She knows that the woman will follow her and will bring others to her underground camp. They will form troops and raid the society thriving below. She cannot move or she will lead the others into doom only to insure her own imagined safety.

Genue waits and resists the urge to flee. The danger will subside. Patience is her only friend. She closes her eyes and daydreams of a time before the world changed. She imagines a time when humans could walk outside at night. There was a time when children could still play in the evening comfort, before humans were hunted. Night was the welcome time to move for the unaltered flesh of society. The past drowns out her present situation and she thinks of a time before now. She closes her eyes and begins to imagine when she was innocent to the tortures of her present reality.

> Genue was the age of six in her memory. Her golden hair defied any attempts her mother forced to contain it. Her smile lit the room. Tonne dropped her arms to her side. There would be no braid today. She gave up the battle and released the child to play once more. Time must no longer be wasted. She would meet with Emila on that night. Tonne knew that there was a great importance about that meeting. Emila found her. She sent word for her. There was something that needed to be discussed and she wanted to see the girl.

The sun receded below the horizon and Tonne escaped outside with her daughter. They walked the mile together to the edge of the river. It was dark and the fog slithered down to the Earth's surface. The ocean would drink that night.

There she stood. The woman. Genue remembered her face of warmth. She appeared to be much older than Tonne. The curious child looked to her mother who was talking to the woman. The innocent little girl, unaware of the information exchanged, retreated back into her thoughts of dolls and make-believe.

Genue is awakened. She can only remember to that point. Frustrated, she pulls her body from under the bench. Her vine is withered and gray. Dead. Genue aborted its existence when she realized she was not alone. The woman is gone by now.

Genue walks back to her fortress. Her ladder, Rapunzel's hair, leads her the way back to her solitude. Genue decides not to tell Tonne of the malfunctioned person she saw outside. Her mother worries that she will be discovered. She is so protective of the girl. As she drifts into sleep she thinks of the life she created in the soil. Genue smiles to herself as she thinks of all that she can do with this new endowment. She has realized her greatest gift.

-THE GOLDEN RULER-

Imaginings of grander,
Lead to the collapse of the frail mind.

At thirteen, Sathe is the Golden Ruler. He is the underground leader of the black market for Biolarity. He meets with Dr. Edextrous. From the time the doctor learned that he is alive, they have been meeting in secret, extracting Sathe's life matter, for a trade of course. There is nothing in this world to be had for free.

Sathe's chlorophyll plasma is the most desired substance to those of afford, with minimal side affects; as opposed to the current remedy, Nanotechnology, with drastic side effects. The affluent buy the chlorophyll plasma in pill form. One gram of his life matter is enough to keep a human from experiencing the effects of the sun for a month. It is a lucrative business. When the asylum is put up for public auction that year, Sathe works a deal with the old doctor.

They discuss a trade of his plasma in exchange for his freedom. It is a shot in the dark, but worth a try. Sathe imagines an underlying bonus: he will have at his disposal an army of rejects willing to do anything. He will be a ruler, their leader. He plans to exploit their foolishness for his own gain.

The doctor enters the monster's concrete fortress. He studies Sathe and contemplates murdering him now. This world would be better if it is rid of the malicious celebrity, the vampire of emotion feeding on the fear of demise. The money is too great for the doctor to end the evil one's existence. People will pay anything to wander the streets with the sun.

Sathe smirks at the doctor who is wearing a leather suit and mask. This is a false since of security, an elementary defense against the poison: the snake's venom.

> Sathe, I have come to talk to you about your freedom. So...you know that leaving this compound is not an option. All the red tape surrounding that boy and Emila, you just can't leave. Nevertheless, there is a building on top of this place, a penthouse of sorts, if you are interested.

> I'll take it. Can we go now? I am tired of looking at this sullen room. It's too dark in here and there is not enough sunlight for my comfort.

The old doctor motions for the guards to collect Sathe's belongings. They pack away his books, most of which are about horticulture, a few philosophy articles, and some science books. He requires minimal clothing. Sathe wears his skin like a fine couture, proud of his distention, now that he is free from his mother's shameful eyes.

Sathe absorbs the moisture from the old leaky pipes running the length of his room, noxious water slowly tainting his cells. He is ready for a change, a new scene to view and count his days as they pass. Now he can plan his vengeance against her, the perfect one.

He plans his exit from the chaos of his life.

Once the guards have gathered the contents of the room, Sathe is chained and walked like a dog down the barren hallway. He leads the path to his new solitude with the slight illusion of freedom. They walk up the six flights of stairs to the top of the building. He can feel the warmth of the sun beating on the tarred roof before they even reach the highest level of his new home. The doctor has no idea of Sathe's newest project: wings. This fortress will never contain him. It will never stop his ultimate escape. This, a rouse, can only last so long.

> This is as far as I will go with you. The sun is overhead forcing us to remain indoors. I'm sure you will be just fine though. We will meet here in a few days. I will need more of your plasma. Do you want to ask me anything, Sathe?

Challenged, Sathe looks back at the old doctor, glaring at him with indignity. He pulls his neck against the chain. *One more victim to execute.*

> *Can I kill you now Doc or maybe at our next visit?*

This question dances around in his mind. He wishes to add another notch on his revenge list. Smiling, licking his teeth, pausing, noticing...no shield to cover the eyes. What a stupid mistake, thoughtless, one that will cost the doctor his life. Sathe laughs out loud.

> Hey Doc, what fun this has been. I want to thank you in advance for my life and this opportunity to shed some light on this situation. Have you enjoyed your time on Earth? It is so sad to end it this way.

Confused, the doctor steps away as the monster kicks the massive door to the roof open. Sunrays splash into the stairwell as Sathe drinks in his power through his pores. The doctor and his two guards are frozen by fear. Verdant sap inundates the diminishing presence of oxygen. An emerald mist radiates from Sathe's venomous body, wrapping his casualties in an inescapable coil of death.

Sathe is pleased. The metal aiding his imprisonment melts and falls to the ground. Earthly compounds are no match to his acid venom. He points his hands toward the mangled bodies slowly suffocating, unable to move on their own. From his fingertips vines sprout, winding and wrapping around the men. He pulls them further onto the roof, now in the direct sunlight.

Sathe inhales the bitter aroma of slowly cooking flesh. He watches as the meat peels away and what was once a human carcass is now a skeleton, void of life. Satisfied, he walks away from the stack of decaying matter. He looks to his star, his only friend in this world, now his only companion.

The green aura of death surrounds Sathe's body, a phenomenon that was discovered by Emila when he was a mere toddler. She was stricken to her bed for a week for holding the boy in her arms after he was exposed to sunlight. The sun's rays escaped the curtain as she walked past. As the ultraviolet particles stroked his skin, a fog surrounded them both. His poison was revealed, however, not fully activated at that time. Now that he has matured, he is lethal.

Sathe looks at his penthouse positioned in the center of the roof. He walks inside. The building is empty except for a chair in the corner covered with stacked newspapers. The room appears as though it was a look out some time ago, a time before the sun swelled and when humans could live outdoors.

Windows serve as walls, painted as a means to block the enemy. The cracked paint flakes off into the air allowing light to enter. Sathe walks to the nearest wall of glass and scratches the covering with his wooden claws. He wants as much sunlight as he can get inside. He grins and circles the room once more.

> This will be my home. I will lure her here and this will be where I take her life, just as they wanted mine after her birth. I will then rule this Earth! No human can stop me from spreading my seed of rot across this planet!

A rustle. The chair in the corner moves. Sathe turns to the commotion. He is not alone. He did not notice before that behind the curtain is a man hiding. Sathe tears down the cloak. Flinching, the man holds his breath.

Who Are You! Who Sent You! Did She?

I am Jubrock! I live here. I mean you no harm. I just want peace.

How do you walk out here with the sun all around?

Nano, I am a nano. Please don't kill me. I will do what you wish. I just want to remain here. I have nowhere else to go.

Sathe studies the figure, obviously deranged, however, his large meaty build is able to withstand the sun thanks to his Nanotechnology. The man is possibly useful but he is most defiantly in need of some personal hygiene.

I am a killer so don't get too close to me. Don't talk to me or ask me any questions. This is my home now. You can live in the stairwell or something.

What a delightful discovery, his first minion to carry out the dirty work of finding his sister. The minute details of mayhem and the path to destruction stand just outside his reach. Sathe delivers his plan to his companion.

First, dispose of those human remains by the door. Then find some water and bathe in it. I will also need a troll of some sorts, a man of questionable morals. Not you. I have plans for you to work around here. I'm thinking a trap door. Anyway, get out of my sight. You smell like a sewer.

Jubrock hunches as he walks away, insecure of his beastly stature. He looks at the pile of what once was alive that is now in decay, then glances back at Sathe with apprehension of what this future relationship will bring. He saw the murder of those men. What else is the freak capable of? He decides not to anger the beast and will see this assignment through.

Jubrock knows of the perfect candidate for Sathe's request, a malingerer who owes him a favor. He lives in dumpsters as a scavenger of society. They were once friends but now enemies. He deserves this stress also. Jubrock leaves the roof, dragging the skeletons behind him. He doesn't realize the many bodies that will continue to fall at the hand of Sathe's reign.

Back in his new fortress, Sathe pulls his worn book from his back pocket. It is the only thing that matters to him. His biography. He dumps the stack of newspapers from the chair onto the floor and drags his throne across the room. He positions it in front of the exposed window and sits into the worn cushion. Sathe props his feet on the sill of the window and thumbs the pages until he finds his favorite entry, the page that is about Tonne, his biological mother. Taking in a deep breath, he begins to read the passage that he has started so many times before.

I met with Tonne today. I saw the girl. She is an angel on this Earth. I know she is good, unlike this monster I am now stuck to endure. He screams at night and long into the day. I don't know what to do. I found Tonne so I could see the girl myself. I wanted to know if she is malfunctioned like the boy. I am assured she is not.

Tonne looked so dragged down. She has traveled underground protecting the child that is her charge. For six years she has remained in hiding. I still can't figure out what she is doing that I am not. I took a picture of the girl. It was dark of course. Tonne is biologically unaltered so she can only move outside at night.

The girl's blond bouncy ringlets were tarnished bronze. What a shame, I wanted to bring her home and give her a bath. Hygiene is so important. I am distressed that a creature worth billions lives among the worthless ranks of society, associating with those unable to afford to live in the daylight.

I was disgusted with Tonne. Her smell. Her dirt. A slum. I told her of the boy. I told her that the girl's brother is the polar opposite of her and that he looks like an orchid with his long body. His white head looks like a budding flower.

I also told her of his temper: his rage. I wanted to warn her of his presence. She was devastated to know that another soul was created from her DNA. I have only added more to her confusion. I assured her that he is confined to our home. He remains indoors, afraid of what the sun may feel like. Of course these are the lies I have told him to keep him complacent with his surroundings. I fear he will overtake my own authority if I allow him the nourishment of the luminous celestial body.

Tonne asked me to let her see him. She wanted to see the boy made from her. I know she wants to show him love. That's all she knows. Stupid love. Like that will change anything. No one can love Sathe. Anyone who gets close to him becomes sick and bedridden. He must be kept at a distance always.

She cried, begging me to let her see him. Pathetic. I mean I didn't even have to tell her about him. A lot of good it did me, abrading my face in the reality that I saved the wrong one. The girl is so refined, so beautiful. I told her never to tell Genue of her brother; that she would only try to find him. I also told her of the reason his life was to be terminated.

When the girl was first created we put her in the same incubation room as the boy. They were in tanks across from each other. That night we locked up as usual, leaving the two budding babies in the confines of the lab.

The next morning, when we arrived back at work, both tanks were a tangle of broken glass and twisted metal. The babies were in the middle of the room on the floor shivering in the cold of the gathered water around them. When we came closer to the bodies we could see that a fiber was winding tightly around the girl, choking the life from her. The labyrinth of matter was a root growing from the boy's fingertips, strangling the innocent one. As we cut her free from the boy's clutches he screamed in pain. The girl was saved and the boy was sentenced to death. I explained to her that the siblings must never meet. The boy will surely take her life. Genue must never know that he exists. Pure evil. Born evil. Die evil.

Sathe looks up from the journal. Emila's words are correct. He does intend to kill Genue, in time. However, he wants the moment to be right. Sathe stands from his throne and watches his new first mate, Jubrock, drag the empty carcasses across the field. He is a perfect slave, already scared into obedience. They have much work to do together preparing his castle for her arrival, the place of her final rest: her death. Contempt is his closest friend, basking in the glory of destruction.

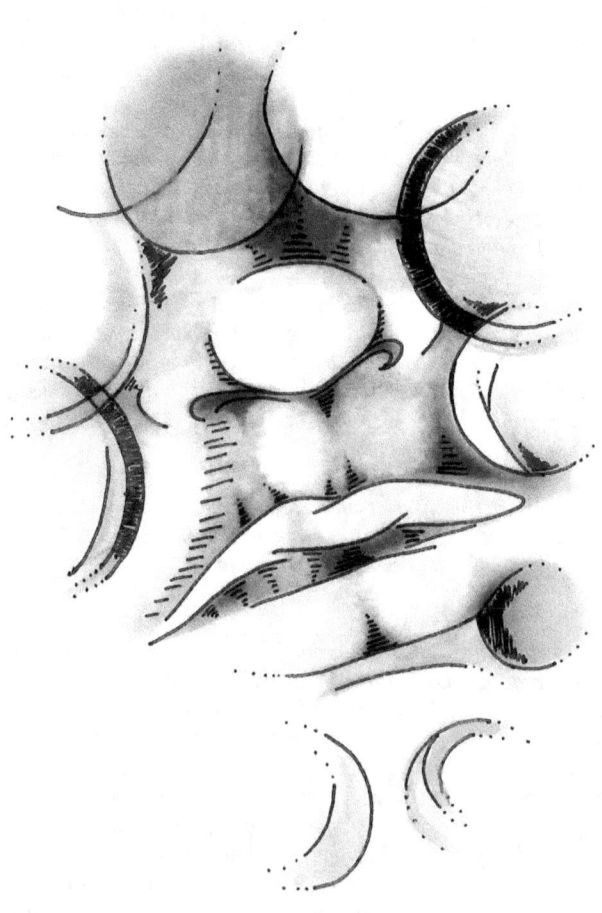

-The Hangman's Sacrifice-

Time allows no escape,
The prisoner must wait.
None to hear her cries at night,
She imagines a day when all is right.

There is no mercy for the hangman's daughter as she sits in the condition of her consequence. She stares deep into his green slit eyes for a remnant of compassion for her soul. The reptiles wish for her death. They know what she has done to betray their tribe.

> Tia, you may choose death for your treasons or you may choose exile. Of course, death is a blessing from your father. He wishes to protect you from the suffering my people want to impose on you.

The blade presses hard into her outstretched neck. The Dragon King is here to punish his wife. She has laid with the morning star and bore his offspring into existence. Tia returns to thoughts of her arms around his neck, the passion of their touch. She would never feel those feelings for her arranged husband and her body shudders in disgust at the thought.

My son will find me in banishment. He will be the future king of our realm. You fear Essuel, and for that you are right. You know that if you kill me now he will kill you later, along with all of your kind. My son will hear my cries. Do what you must to me. He will find me!

That, we shall see, Tia Mea, Queen of Diaspora, we shall see if he will come to save you from your *PENANCE!*

+ + + + + + +

The banished queen remembers the last moments before her exile. She sits in the corner of her prison, all alone. Her surroundings are the cancer of her time, wasting away in solitude, the trade for her life. Her walls of existence are barren. She resides on the Plutonian moon, Kerberos, void of light. Silence is her only companion. Hid away, she is right beneath her son's grasp.

Tia watches the starseed fairies dance in the chill motion of the celestial sphere. Her father rules the skies, as the reigning Dragon Emperor. He controls the fifth dimension gate, a responsibility granted his bloodline from the beginning of time. He has corrupted in his older age and allows none to enter. He throws the starseeds back into the three-dimensional loop where they repeat the cycle indefinitely.

The Monarch's prized daughter, Tia, was to join the dragon tribes across the universe and end the dissention between the families of reptiles and become allies against the humanoid ones, the Inogenue. He is the enemy, Essuel's father. She saw him that day on the empty stellar highway of the photon belt. Their love was instant.

But what if our union could join and end the war. Our love would end the tension that lies between our nations.

He tucks her loosely curled hair behind her ear and kisses her softly on the lips as he smiles at her innocent request. She is naive to the underlying current of the hostility within the situation.

> Tia, it is not part of their plan. We will both die of treason and your father will give the dragon king your sister instead. The reptiles need the war against the Inogenue. They will never defeat us though, because we were created by the source of spiritual passion. One who lives his life with intensity and desire will have a divine journey. Tia, we must never come forward.

> My beautiful man, I am afraid we cannot hide our love any longer. We are with child. We must tell the joy of our union!

She remembers the look on his face. A look of panic, his crumbling desire for the situation. She felt the distance that day. He would never hold her the same. She knew this was her burden to carry.

> You must seduce your husband to be. They will murder us both. Tia, I need you to forget me. I cannot go with you any farther.

> But I thought you loved me! We started this affair together.

> Tia, I fell for your beauty but I have been promised to another wife. I will not abandon my promise to her.

+ + + + + + +

Tia balls her mangled confidence within her frail body. The loneliness of her days in exile has worn her down. Her only strength comes from knowing her son is still calling out to her. She can feel his heart beating along the currents of the stellar highway.

A starseed fairy lands on her knee. She studies its radiance. A light emits from its delicate wings. The queen encourages the tiny creature to stay by reaching her hand to it and plucking it from her leg. She brings the seed to her lips and places a kiss on its wing before biting it into the fire of flesh. The seed screams in horror as Tia welcomes the nourishment into her empty core. Her skin glows golden hues as she digests the fire within.

Essuel was born a humanoid. She could not deny his paternity. His golden skin and piercing grey eyes, a stark contrast to the illuminated flesh of the dragon with razor slit eyes and skin like mother of pearl.

> Tia! What have you done? This boy is not mine! He is not from the Order of the Dragon! He is a mortal!

She never said a word to him of Essuel's lineage. Her husband already learned the purpose of the boy's birth in the divine plan of the universe. A dream revealed to him an epiphany the night before the arrival of the child. His mental picture was of a comet with a fire trailing for miles, an entity that was sent to infiltrate his master plan. The king knew she had fallen for the morning star.

Tia pulled the boy to her chest and caressed his golden tufts of hair as she comforted his cries into her breast. She spoke to him one last time. She held him tight to her chest as she laid her final words in his ear.

> *My sweet innocent son, I will protect you as long as I remain. I have taught you all I know so that one day you will carry my blood into war and demolish the soul loop that has created the rot of our happiness. You will grow to be a warrior and the King knows that you will defeat him. Do not fear him my child, for you hold all the power of life in your hands. Never forget the lessons I have taught you. It is a potential you will carry into your rule of this universe one day.*

This was her last whisper to her beloved boy. It was also her last moment to lay her eyes on his cherub face. She smeared a tear across his forehead and kissed his young hand before handing him over to his father to escape.

Never forget where you came from. You are the Dragon. You were made to kill the Inogenue.....

-ALTERING THE REALITY-

She enters the tunnel leaving her past behind.
Memories pound into her thoughts as she
escapes the form she was once confined.

Essuel.......Essuel my son.....come to me....bathe
in my love my boy.....do what you know must be
done to protect our creation...our legacy carried
into the future.

Essuel sits up from his dream. His mother was there, the dragon queen. He relaxes and lies back down, resting his head on folded arms. He knows it is time to enter the physical dimension. It is time to intervene. Tonne has been distracting him from this day. She is just afraid of the spirit canal. She is afraid of the cross over, although, she knows it is the only way to enter three-dimensional life. Tonne has chosen to plant the seed for love by entering the flesh. Unfortunately, there must also be the balance of hate even if only to make the force of love stronger. Essuel drifts back to sleep. Tomorrow will be the day they change the world.

The next evening Essuel leads Tonne back to his room of history. He has prepared her a place to rest. Her fourth dimensional shell will remain here after she has crossed over. Essuel will never return to this cavern once the mission has begun. He will escape into the ether until his time on the surface is needed. Tonne looks into his eyes, pleading for another way. He helps her to the ground one last time.

Essuel! I am nervous. What if it doesn't work right or if I can't cross over and possibly I go into an unwanted figure...I am so scared...

Tonne, this is the only way. We can only effect change if we too are in the flesh as they are. The project has gone completely wrong. We must intervene now or all that we have created will forever be lost.

But what if I forget my mission? I must start as a baby. What if I forget everything I have known and I live a completely void life and not on course and....

Tonne, stop this! You will throw the project if you keep your vibrational frequency on this low thought process. I have plans of keys that will unlock your mission hidden deep within your brain. I will be with you in dreams and you will know me within your subconscious thoughts.

Will you miss me Essuel? Will you miss my warmth? My love? Will you move on with your life without me?

Tonne, I will never leave your side. You will not see me but you will know me. When you see the call for volunteers for an experiment named Biolarity, you will lead yourself to me. You will know instinctively that you are the only one who can make the study work.

But how will I know Essuel? I don't even know what Biolarity is now. How will I know what it is then?

You will just know. Please be calm my love. You must learn your path in dreams. I will see you again and you will know me.

Essuel presses his hand into Tonne's chest. He must stop her heart. He must throw her seed into the spirit canal and give it life on the physical plain. She will not know him after this moment. She slips into the collected consciousness under his fingertips.

Essuel stands and looks into the darkened sky. Only when the moon is aligned with the sun can he end her existence in the Venetian shell she wears as of now. Her radiating gold skin of crystal will be turned into the soft mud of human flesh.

Essuel watches the sun rise slowly into the morning atmosphere. He sits with his thoughts of loosing his delicate Tonne forever. She will be thrown from his enchantment. He fears she will never remember him. He stands and walks back to his lovely bride. She is dreaming. He needs her in this state of peace to learn her life ahead. She must go over in her mind the locks that require keys of understanding.

Behind is a stir. He is not alone.

Oh Essuel! You thought this would be done so easily. Your arrogance astonishes me brother! Here I am to step in and finish this tragedy…

Annuil! How did you find me here? I will not let you take this from me! I will have what I want! I will have the star system and you will only be but a fleck of matter meaning nothing to anything. Just as you deserve!

Why Essuel, are you still upset that father loves me and not you? Must be a terrible feeling being a bastard to the king. Royal but worthless!

Essuel takes the bait and bites hard. He flies into Annuil's body throwing them both into the cavern wall. The cave shakes with the impact of the brother's combined force of hate. Annuil struggles to free himself from Essuel's clutches while receiving three blows to the eye. Agony sets in as he stumbles onto his knees. He is pushed back onto the ground and Essuel stands tall above him.

> Annuil, you will never be as strong as I am!
> You will never defeat the Dragon King as I am.
> You are just an intolerant rival fighting for the
> throne that you will never sit upon. You toss
> pebbles while I throw stones!

Essuel spits onto the ground by his traitor brother's face. At the opening of the cavernous room he sees a shadow dance across the surface of the sun. The eclipse has begun. He runs over to Tonne who is deep into the tangle of delirium. He pulses his hand over her mouth encouraging her soul into his fingertips. Golden hues escape her lips. Essuel kisses her face one last time before her essence explodes into molten air circling her body. He closes his eyes in the brightness of the surrounding particles. Essuel throws her soul into the tunnel emerging and growing all around them. The light strokes her spirit and disappears. Tonne is gone. She will be born flesh.

Annuil finds a large rock on the ground beside him. Standing from the floor, he launches his accomplice through the air and into Essuel's head. He tackles his brother to the ground and pounds the side of his face with the stone. Essuel falls in and out of consciousness.

> Tonne may be born, but you will never be there
> to guide her! You will die here tonight Essuel!
> She will be alone and I will find her! I will kill
> her and your mission will be in ruins!

Essuel closes his eyes. She made it. He can feel her entering the womb. He begins to drift into the fog. His last image is of Annuil smiling down at him, rolling his tongue across his teeth and tasting the blood of his nemesis on his lips. Annuil turns from his brother and walks out of the cavern.

Darkness creeps into the obscurity of Essuel's existence. Annuil did not succeed in killing his brother. The war will continue on, fed a rich diet of disparity and indignation. Essuel places his hand upon the gaping wound above his eye. A scar will remain to advise him of the betrayal by his kin. He remembers her pass into the third dimension. She will walk with the humans. She will bring forth the healer who will stop the swollen orb from burning their precious offspring.

White! Pink! Blue! Flashes of ultraviolet light surround her soul, freed of its ethereal containment. Tonne has entered the flesh. She will begin her mission to save the humans from the blistering orb of fire, conceived by her lover's grasp. Tonne will make the Biolarity a concrete actuality of existence. Only an Inogenue can bring forth the change. Her starseed enters the travail path to the mortal presence and penetrates the spiritual chord. She will incarnate into an infant avatar to complete her soul contract. No memories to consort with. No past to forget. All fresh. Tonne is born.

Essuel walks over to the place on the floor where her form once laid. He presses his hands onto the hard earth where she will never be again. He looks around the room at the paintings covering the walls. He remembers showing her this room, his cavern of secrets, before life became so confusing.

Essuel cries tears into his hands and rubs the moisture into the stone walls. New art emerges depicting his present scene. He tells the story of the Judas kiss. He imagines her soul floating above her anatomy and exiting into the canal to her upcoming birth. He weeps. Essuel has lost Annuil and now his lady. His brother, the one he must assassinate, and the other he longs to love again, to create the space for love and hate. This is what the Inogenue want. The balance must be returned to order. This is why his life was made. This is why the dragons merged with the humanoid beings. There will be balance among the chaos. Without the balance, our universe will be destroyed.

-Evil is at the Door-

*She must trap his contempt
and contain his rage,
Her brother, Sathe,
lost amongst the piles of decay.*

*Sixteen. What a wonderful age.
Full of promise for the youthful soul.
I sit atop my prolific empire I have created.
I look around my greenhouse.
Windows freed of their covers.
The sunlight is welcome.
Orchids. My mother's orchids.
I had them shipped here after her. . . untimely death.*

Each flower vibrates as he walks by and grazes his fingers across the surface, encouraging the petals to bow at him in honor. Sathe smiles at his subjects, his ancestors, relatives. As he turns to walk away, his black coat slaps the flowers back into submission, this being his cruelty. He loves the orchids and hates them at the same time, just as he does his sister. He loves that he is not alone. He hates that she will always be better than he is. Genue must die. Jubrock will find her and Sathe will destroy her.

Genue awakens. Why can she not move? She feels that her body is trapped. She is bound to a stretcher and is being pulled behind something. By the up and down motion she determines that it is someone. She remembers her mother's burning body as the flame carefully caressed her remains. She remembers the feeling that crept over her when she realized that she was not alone.

Tears escape Genue's eyes and soak into the cloth that is binding her to the board. She is responsible for this mission alone and she is without the guidance of her mother to lead her down the correct path. She feels her present condition tighten its hold on her psyche.

Followed, stalked, and abducted. A man hit her and has captured her. Her body is covered and hidden like luggage. She tries to pull her arms away from her but she is tied, wrapped, and bound. Genue saves her fight for later. Her powers would free her from the Earthly chains. The decision to rest creeps into her mind and she is lulled to sleep by the thudding of the ground underneath. As she sleeps she dreams within the trail of her unconscious thought. A voice calls out to her.

Though inscape seems the course,
Beware of your chances.
If your gut tells you something,
It is us guiding you in dances.

Genue is in the whiteness of an alter reality. She can feel it around her, seeping into her wilted soul. There is no body. Only white. A static ripples in front of her as a face emerges from the light. It is one that is familiar to her.

Mother is that you? But you are dead.

Yes, my daughter, I have returned to tell you of the great mission you must complete. The Earth is depending on you to save it from the destruction by the source of your creation.

Tonne marvels at the strength burning within Genue. The responsibility to save the balance of nature is a great task. Noticing the confusion in her daughter's eye, Tonne explains the direction of reality further.

> *Your brother is an insect. He must be squashed, but he is hardly your greatest task. There will be a war, a deeper conflict than anything ever known to man. You will lead the army to save this Earth and rid the presence of the machine. I must go now. I have a new destination. I will see you again my lovely daughter. My soul will live on through you.*

A tear within the static ripples down Genue's cheek. She wipes it away, smearing her emotion back into her flesh. Tonne smiles at her daughter, knowing the truth of her existence, the love for Planet Earth, to save it from the solar flame. To be saved will also lead to the destruction of many.

> *Gen, soon this will all mean nothing. You will change and become your purpose, free to choose your own path. Free to love.*

The static returns as Genue notices the cold returning to her skin. She sees her mother for the last time, fading into the frost of the white nothingness.

> **Don't be afraid, it is he who should be scared.**
> **Our tolerance is over, for he has much to demand.**
> **He will learn love, but will remain trapped.**
> **Ceased, but still alive.**

Genue watches the face of her mother slip away into the distant space surrounding her. She begins to loose her footing and she falls from the collected consciousness. She slips into the tethered dream, pulling herself back into the light of her present reality. Her eyes open to a bolt of light. Jubrock, her captor, stumbles. There is someone else out there. Genue feels trouble setting in. She hears his frightened voice speak into the night:

What are you? I can't see your face. Move that light!

THUNK! Thud! Slerp!

Genue can feel the stretcher move again. She can feel the stranger's aura. The energy is not of this Earth or even of this reality. Possibly alien. Unknown. Unidentified. Genue smells the element of sulfur in the air, the excretion, as it overtakes all other aromas. <u>They</u> have intervened. <u>They</u> changed the story. <u>They</u> are not supposed to do that. She must be special.

The conflicting entity plays a new perception in Jubrock's mind, an existence of giving rather than taking. Love. Pure love. Genue feels their presence all around. Her body burns with longing to hold them and touch them, the Inogenue. She feels them leave. Jubrock is like someone new, humming and singing. Her keeper feels joy. She will make him feel pain later. She must escape captivity. Today is not her judgment day.

Genue breathes the dry listless air. By the agility of her toes, she opens the bottom of the cloth and with each bump on the path, she slips further down on the board. Genue takes a deep breath and exhales, reducing her size, and slides from the entrapment of the gurney. Jubrock doesn't notice her escape until she trips on her steps. He looks back and before he can fully turn his head, she swings the bar into his face.

BLONK!   CRACK!   Thu-ud!

Unconsciousness washes over his thoughts.
The light inside dims and he is thrown
into his darkest secrets.

Jubrock feels his own thoughts drift as he falls to the ground. His assertions take over the aura of the room, uncomfortable and at once undesired. Time reverses further into his dreams with each passing second. When his body makes contact he knows he is within his darkest thoughts. Strangely, his past feels much like his current situation.

Jubrock is there with Claira, his wife. He remembers her soft golden hair, long and light as air. He smiles as he remembers her honey-hued shoulders. Thoughts of touching her, reassuring her that she would be well again soon, cross his mind. Jubrock watches himself, stationed in a memory, an impression from the past; dancing around, taunting him with imagined abilities to change what is about to occur.

Jubrock is standing at the doorway of the house he shared with his wife. He can smell her sweet essence in the air, inviting him to experience more while he watches her standing in the center of the room, her back turned to him. She is crying. He knows this from the way her shoulders are moving, jerking to the beat of her sobs. As she turns, Jubrock screams into the walls of his purgatory to stop the torment of his memory. She turns to her husband and he can see her face, the reason for her sadness. Her skin, once of porcelain beauty, is now a nightmare flashing back through his mind, taunting him with her remaining flesh of stone. The black coldness of the hardened clay, immortalizing her pain as smoke escapes where there was once breath. Her frame crumbles to the ground, sinking deep into the recesses of his worst thoughts.

+ + + + + + +

Jubrock opens his eyes and Claira is gone. The nightmare disappears and his physical presence is restored. He returns to his new reality, now the captive, at the mercy of the orchid.

> Get up and walk! I know who sent you to find
> me. Now I want you to take me to my brother!

Jubrock collects his being and begins to walk ahead of Genue. Her skin changes from blue to gold. He tries to glance from the side of his eyes to see her. She is the one who has over taken him. It is as though his mind and body are numb by her powers, her energy. He possesses no struggle or desire to be free. He is her prey. Jubrock is on autopilot as he takes her straight to Sathe's lair. He is a map, a guide to her destiny. She speaks in a soft whisper. Gentle.

> So how do you know my brother? And why
> has he sent you to find me and not himself?

In response to her question, Jubrock stumbles over his steps, throwing his brain back into the present state of discussion.

> Oh, um. . . Sathe is my boss, I guess. He makes me do evil things. I don't know why I am saying these words. Your force is pulling the truth from my lips. What are you? Will you make me do evil things too? Are you all the same?

Jubrock knows that Genue is nothing like Sathe. He knows that she is innocent in this tortuous situation. However, the question still knocks at his insecurities. What will she do to him?

> Never mind that. Why does my brother want me dead? I only learned of his existence moments before my mother's death, so I didn't get any details. As you saw, I laid her body to rest.

Jubrock says nothing. He doesn't know what Sathe's plans are for his sister except that he wants her dead. He remembers the flame he found Genue by, the burning embers. He didn't know who was sent back to the dust, but seeing the girl's tears it must have been someone she loved. He knows of loss. Remaining alive, as the one you love escapes into the clouds of the spirit world, is torture.

Silence.
The perpetrator of awkward. The mastermind of discomfort.
Understood by no one. Experienced by everyone.

Silence. Jubrock, unsure of himself, gawks at her cultivation of presence. He thrashes at his knowledge, searching for a way to complete the conversation with her. She seems jaded, untouchable, like a wounded elephant that never forgets the wrong done to it.

> So how'd ya say your mother died?

His question came out before he could contain it. He could read the shift in the air that this topic was not one of discussion. Genue looks back at him. What is with this curiosity? Why does he even care?

> *I killed her for my survival. My mother was sacrificed, so that the one she was in charge to protect, at all costs. . .could live.*

A figurative wall of emotion falls and crashes all around her. Genue watches as all her guilt, resentment, and her fears, crumble to her feet. She weeps.

> I killed my mother. That is all. It had to be done. She wouldn't have it another way. She was stubborn like that and in the end she sacrificed her own life for mine.

> *I proceed with my mission.*
> *Tonne met her destiny.*

Jubrock walks faster. Is she worse than her brother? Or is she the one to save us all from him. Sathe is hatred, insecurities, and revenge. Genue is love, passion, and grace. Jubrock looks back at her again. Innocence. Exquisite. He wonders if he could hide away with her. Genue could pass for machine. Jubrock is a Nano. He imagines leading her through the jungle of civilization, on a wild goose chase. Sathe would find her though.

Ahead lies a fork in the road. To go left: safety, intelligence, the city. To the right: Sathe's palace, asylum, the penthouse. They walk together through the forest of disorder and chaos. Genue remains one step behind to insure that Jubrock doesn't try to escape. He asks, barely a whisper.

So do you kill people you touch like your brother does?

He doesn't really want to know. It doesn't matter. He hopes she didn't hear his question after all. Genue ponders his question for a moment. Over the years, all sixteen of them, she supposes that she has only brought about positive change. Healing, love, and beauty, added to her world. She heals the wounded and tired. She creates life, the polar opposite of what her brother does. Except for the eye she took. Leerah's eye. The mistake. The evil. Karma will tighten its hold, finding the perfect moment to strike. Genue will pay for what she did to that girl's face.

Yea, I hurt people, so don't test me.

Jubrock stops. Genue stops. Ahead she sees the asylum. He took her to the right. It is her destiny. She must now continue forward.

Black decay. Modern design.
Old fashioned. Out of date. Decrepit.

Two men stare at them from in front of the gated entrance; the structure that patiently secures the monster living within its walls. It provides a false safety protecting their ignorance.

Whispers and flutters. . .the Nano breakdown.
The mental disintegration of the first edition.
Scientists. Doctors. Elite. Early test runs.
They were willing to experiment, but are now a ruin.

Casualties of Science, the human sacrifice, the result of the malfunction of microscopic computers contained within the host body. Slowly, the cancer erodes the cellular structures at the most basic level, within the bloodstream, that induces the birth of a zombie nation. They roam the grounds of the ward, living off wildlife, strangers, and drifters: the lost and forgotten of this existence. Genue's heart seems to stop. Sathe is here. He is close to her. She can feel him.

His lair: tower on the roof.
A green house: the orchid shrine.

Energy vibrates through the particles in the air. He is near. Her pulse trembles and causes her heartbeat to race high. She feels her other polarity, her opposite, the perfect match, classified as: *male/plant dominant vs. female/plant recessive.*

Genue looks for him. Through the windows of his tower above, she sees him. She watches him as he turns away into his secrecy. She will meet him soon. Biolarity. Genue grabs the flint rocks from her pocket and strikes them upon one another. Spark! Her skin ignites. Jubrock turns to see her flesh turn to fire. Her hair begins to flicker and flame, with bright all around. Sathe sees the flash in the night sky. He runs back to the window. *It is her! She is here!*

Sathe runs to the door and into the darkness. He sees her standing across the yard. She is fire and he is ice. Jerking at the ties of his coat for freedom, he struggles to release his body. The black of night is now his only cloak. His skin is revealed. From his back, wings splay out, growing, building cell upon cell, until completion. His Nanotechnology creation combined with his biological power, something he has been working on. His fresh additions stretch to the wingspan of that of an albatross.

Genue sees Sathe, mighty like a dragon, the one who wants her life. This is who she has been running and hiding from her entire life? Her pounding heart and screaming thoughts distract her mind from the trance of delirium and extinguishes the flame of her body. She drops the rocks and her hair fades. Drained and tired, grayed from the stress of her upcoming battle, she is weakened on her feet. It will be hours until her golden youth returns.

Genue must hide one final time, until the full sun is her ally. She looks above at the skeleton trees. She can blend into the branches and rest. Genue disappears into the tallest tree. She hides above, having no below. He saw her; whatever he is. She knows he will come for her. Sathe looks below where his closest relative once stood. She is a powerful opponent. Her core of fire will be a close match to his sap of destruction. She appears to be gone for now, but he knows she will return.

> She knows I saw her and will think I am coming for her. Of course I am but I will wait until daylight returns, when my powers are at their greatest. I will rid the world of her and complete my plan for domination. I will kill them all with my poison fingers and feed my soul with their blood!

Pounding chest and his evil smile overtake his body, changing the chore of life into the moment of his rapture. His mission is almost complete. Sathe walks back to his throne. Inside his darkened retreat, he rests to recharge. He reaches behind and detaches the wings from his back. Once removed, a brown wither begins until nothing more than sand remains. A new pair will grow when he sees her again.

In his penthouse he sits and waits for her to resurface. He reaches for the journal on the table beside him. His life has been a lie of hiding behind a false identity. Not any more. People will fear him and know that he is their ruler. He will make the world turn. He smiles, licking his teeth. There will be answers and truth. Above all, there will be revenge. If she had not been created they would have kept him. He was to be the great healer. She was brought into existence, with her perfection, and his dignity was torn from within him. She must die so that he will be special again.

> When it is light of day I will destroy her. I know she is not far. I can smell her disgusting innocence. Enough of this irritating creature, death is all that remains!

Sathe sits with his approaching power and drifts into a deep sleep. A victim in reality, an avatar for the mind as it escapes and mingles with the collected consciousness. He travels the tangles of delirium and explores the trails of imagery, searching for her.

A dream. He believes it is real, not yet realizing that he is in his own imagination: digging around, unearthing his secrets from far below. Within the safety of his thoughts, Sathe hears a voice. A whisper at first, growing into the powerful wail that is now resonating inside his mind.

I am the Inogenue!
Your cause has brought us shame,
and now you will remain.
The site of your purgatory,
watching the world age.
Trapped at their mercy.
Your PENANCE:
Giving life for all eternity,
until the last day.

A hand reaches toward him. Sathe looks up and sees a box with the word "Penance" scratched into the side. As the darkness fades a woman emerges from the shadow of the box. Glowing braids of crimson hair wind around her head. Her turquoise eyes emit a fog of dissimulation. She smiles at him as he receives the box into his own hands.

The woman of mystery blows air from her rose petal lips into his face. Colors of fuchsia are born as her breath mixes with the fog. Sathe looks at a box she has given him. He carefully raises the lid and looks inside. Tiny brown seeds, one no larger than the next, fill the box. Winding its way through the mass, a green vine, resembling a snake, slides over of the side of the wooden enclosure.

Sathe drops the box to his feet. Seeds spill, bounce, and spray into the nothingness, like quarks in the vast sea of a hadron collider. He feels the vine circle his ankles. It winds up the length of his legs and wraps around his arms, arresting him in captivity. Desperate to be free, Sathe screams into the nightmare. The vine chokes his cries, constricting his throat. Dancing in front of his face, the vine spits in his mouth and stabs him in the eyes. He is at once silenced.

+ + + + + + +

Is it safe?

Jubrock looks up into the branches above. He sees her, the body from which the sweetest sound has escaped, shattering the silence. The air around them gasps at the intrusion of her words. All he can do in response is shake his head in complete assurance. Genue jumps from the branch and lands on all four, as a lioness would pounce on her pillage. She sits beside him in the forest of bramble weeds, toiling and turning among the dust and decay. She speaks into the empty surroundings.

So are you the one THEY sent to me?

Yea, I guess I am.

Jubrock is a man of torture. He lost his love, his wife, to the same technology that saved him. The boils erupted from her sweat glands. Bodily fluids coated her skin and caused the gelatinous substance to choke the inner life from her pores. Her remaining matter, solidified, hardened, and turned to metal, the product of the machine. Her once soft skin, reduced to a powder, fell to the ground at her skeleton feet. She died in his arms. The nano-robots traveled fast. His own skin took a drink, swelling and rehydrating, youth and glow, as he watched his lover turn to sand.

I need you to do something for me.

Inside Jubrock's mind: Reality – She speaks. Get out of your head thinking about the past. You can't do anything about what has happened and dwelling on it isn't going to change the story. Get into now – this presence. You just saw this person turn to fire, blazing heat, and you are stuck in the past: your past love. Wake up man! You are in love now – with her. Now listen to what she is saying to you.

He smiles at her as she tucks her hair behind her ear. A demure girl, shy to life, barely aware of who she is, striving to become the woman she was born to be.

> You will go to the old *Eagle's Nest Dinner* building. Once inside, find the door labeled: *Storage Alpha*. Behind is a duct system that will lead you into a tunnel. At the end of the path you will find a door. Tell the voice sensor box that you are a friend of Leerah. You will be let in. Don't ever admit to being a nano or you will be executed.

Jubrock's expression is of confusion. She is leading him to the *Door of the Underworld:* a myth to those living the high life above the surface. There is quite a bounty for he who uncovers this door. His expression is now that of planning, connecting the dots on his method of benefit from this new situation.

> Take my book and keep it hidden. I will come for it. You will die a traitor's death if you are found out. It is the only account of the Biolarity project.

Genue hands her journal to Jubrock. She shakes at the magnitude of trust she is giving him, this man who once wanted to harm her. She can feel Tonne within him. She can feel his good. Genue releases her fear. Jubrock wraps his hands around the book. He notices that it is exactly like the one that belongs to Sathe.

Stay below the surface. My fire will destroy many. I don't want to loose you to my flame. I will find you as soon as I can. What is your name?

I am Jubrock. Yours?

Gen.

Good to meet you Gen. seems we will be on this journey together then. I will do what you ask of me. I will find Leerah.

He stands. Jubrock feels her burning hand inside his skull, altering his perception for her benefit and goes without a fight. Genue watches him walk away into the night. He disappears into the crippled forest of lifeless trees and tumbleweeds. He has begun his journey into the unknown at her request.

Genue turns her focus onto the object of her anger. How long has Sathe been looking for her? She can remember the day they started to hide. The *Underground,* below the surface, a refuge from the sun, became her only measure of safety. She is young in her memory, not old enough to understand. She thinks back to the time of their first escape.

Genue watches as her mother packs two backpacks on the foot of her bed. She can even smell the room of murky dust as her thoughts guide her back into the recollection, her delirium of delight, before her life changed to disparity. She can feel Tonne's elevated heartbeat and anxiety of being trapped within these walls.

Where are we going?

Tonne stops packing and reminds herself to breathe. She has no idea where to go, just far away from the boy she saw today, the orchid boy who spoke to her at the bus stop. How long has he been stalking them, following her at night? Tonne knows that he despises Genue. He has made it clear he means her harm.

> *Baby, I think we are going to have to just go where our paths may take us on this one.*

Genue sits up. An adventure awaits! Finally, life has become so boring, cowering indoors, and only venturing outside at night. She would glow like a match in the daylight. All would discover she is the missing experiment. She doesn't know the journey will lead her further away from the sun. She imagines the last time on the surface, before her mother hid them away in the underground. Beneath the outer crust, all is browned from the decay, even her memories.

Genue thinks of how she felt all those years ago, a child, still innocent and naive to the evil world surrounding her utopia. She remembers the feeling Tonne gave her. Peace. Genue lies down to sleep underneath the skeleton trees. Tomorrow she must confront her terror, the reason for her misery, the journey into her fear.

Night is merely a
        shadow now as
fire burns
        the opposing side.

In constant global distress,
            the smoldering star
    licks the ozone barrier.

There is no line
        of defense against
    the over-indulging
                monster.

Fire forces even the most
            unlikely to sacrifice
    themselves to the
                machine.

-THE STARSEEDS-

The dragon's egg will open,
Freeing the demons to run wild.

Annuil knows his brother is planning to overthrow him. Since his birth, Essuel has been out for blood. Annuil opens his flask bringing the rim to his nose, unleashing the metallic aroma into his nostrils. One sip and he will live forever. He drinks the alchemist's dream, his blood drowning in the metallic liquid delusion, tied to the ethereal realm of the alter reality.

Hot. He feels the fire burning within, displacing the oxygen and consuming his flesh. Gasping for his breath of salvation, Annuil falls to the ground. He can feel his chakras, one by one, burst from within, the pulse of passion igniting each energy point into reaction. All he can see is a flicker of gold on his eyelids before he is cast out into the unconscious delirium, dancing in the requiem of ecstasy. The perfect dream...

My dear boy, Annuil, why so long?

Annuil turns to see his mother standing in front of him. She is her son's raven beauty. Her tresses of ebony silk, tarnished with age and loss of time, grow long past her feet.

Annuil, I need you to listen to me. Your brother is taking the starseeds from the heavens and enslaving their souls on Earth. He plans to never to return them to your father's responsibility. Essuel's mother, a dragon queen, taught him how to harvest light energy and create life. He has successfully created one like the Inogenue. He will torture and destroy the humans. He will turn them over to the machine and then our home will be destroyed. He must be stopped my son. The starseeds must be returned to the cosmos or your father will die and then we will all succumb to the same fate.

Wait mother! He is my brother! Wait! Don't go!

The war is hardly over son. I need you to set this right. Essuel and his bride, Tonne, must die. The Earth must die so that it may be reborn like the phoenix.

But why can't the dragons intervene? I must be the one to betray Essuel and it stings my soul.

Annuil, your brother betrayed us. He abandoned our culture and our way of life by sharing our secrets with the starseeds. Your father wants to live to see the history of our essence set right. He has given you this great task.

Mother where are you going? Please come back to me! I need you here by me!

Annuil watches as her face disappears into the shadow of his intellect. He cries out. She is gone, reduced to the static in the matrix of his subconscious. He is thrown back into the reality of his existence.

Bitter metal. Golden spit.

Annuil fully awakens. He has survived the metal and will now be immortal. He climbs back onto his feet. His skin is golden; shimmery like the scales on a fish. He remembers his mother speaking to him and laying out his mission. Essuel must die. He thinks of all the work that lies ahead of him. There can be no mistake. Annuil runs his tongue across his teeth, a habit he has grown to rather enjoy.

-INTRODUCTIONS ARE MADE-

When they meet. . . .
The passion. The love, The hate.
One that only time could obliterate.

Amid the cold October sky, saddened by the loss of innocence, the trees break and crumble to the ground. The surrounding atmosphere sinks into her open pores. Genue can feel the pounding heart of Mother Earth burning under her feet.

The sun is scolding her child, punishing the young planet for allowing such a bitter twist of fate. The father is upset with his creation. It is time to welcome the phoenix to the grave. Genue feels the moment of her purpose, the calming of her inner tide, has materialized.

Sathe awakens, surrounded by blistering light. It is now day. He walks to the window and sees Genue standing in the center of the field. He hears her voice calling to him within the synopsis of his mind.

What do you want from me?
All these years I have crept below,
away from you. I am here now!
Come to me brother!

Sathe falls to the ground as she releases his thoughts. He can feel her pulling him towards her. He feels his breath tearing from his soul. She is powerful. He stands back on his feet and can see her from the window. A blue fog surrounds her body. The sun is pulsing within her aura. Trees ignite into flame. Where there were once branches, now is the animation of heat, an arsonist's wildest dream. The winter changes into summer, leaving behind spring's light dress, a whisper of love before the hate.

Genue can hear the rustle all around. The people, malfunctioning nano-robots and living zombies, are drawn to her energy, wanting to devour her flesh with each pounding beat of her heart. Her fate is star crossed, born of flesh and of immortal fire. She will take the sun in her clutches and calm the angry inferno.

At once, Genue knows what her purpose has been all along. She looks down at her hands, hardened by the stress of time. She is here to save the Earth, bonded to the soil by the orchid, representing the physical domain of power, to absorb the blaze of the nourishing star.

The solar nucleus is off-balance by the external force. Genue does not know who or what the being is that controls the ball of fire. She can feel his masculine energy as he forces his wishes on the fertile crust of life. She will crack the shell today and release the contained energies. She will meet the demon of her fate, the devil in disguise.

Sathe stands on the roof and imagines great wings growing from his back. Like before, his creations emerge from the air. He spreads them out into the atmosphere, now a great dragon, gnashing his teeth, ready to attack his target. His mutation, nano and plant, makes his wings more perfect than her.

Sathe jumps from the safety of his lair and soars into the sky. He is the beast, a sublime fire in the barren sky. Genue stares in amazement at his figure. He lands beside her. Inhale. Exhale. He turns to face her, lowering his wings. Sathe smiles while licking his teeth in satisfaction.

Genue is not impressed or afraid of her brother. She feels at one with herself. Heat rises as her aura brightens. She notices that this creature standing in front of her actually looks like her, as though peering into a mirror, except on the other side is hell.

> I am Sathe! I am your flesh! You were created so that I could be destroyed and so now I intend to kill you! I hate your existence, Genue!!!

She cannot speak. All she can do is breathe. Breathe. Just breathe. These words are planted into her intellect. She follows the cyclical motion of her beating starseed, longing to be released from the physical confinement of the body.

Breathe. As she inhales deeply and exhales with great force, the air around them begins to pulse. Golden auras burn from her skin as embers drip from her nose and ears. Sathe reaches for her arm to stop the hysteria growing around them both. Genue grabs his face with her burning hands! Sathe screams in torment! Green sweat pores from the surface of his skin.

Chlorophyll. Poison. Venom.

The sap of Sathe's flesh slides down his face, over his body, and into the earth below his feet, poison nourishing the soil, sprouting vines that grow in the place of nothing. An ivy wraps around his feet, restricting his movement. Genue digs her nails into his flesh.

The sun reaches for her, caressing her hair, licking her illuminated shell. His worst nightmare, the prophecy, has come true. Sixteen years have passed. He feels the trap tighten. He will remain contained in this crust of his own flesh. He can feel his figure dysfunction as his body mutates into the form of a tree, rippling along his spine.

The hate. The love. The passion is gnashing the sky all around inside the atmosphere. This was meant to bring them together, an exact copy of each other, staring at their own reflections changing and mutating into one another. Genue pulls the molten air around them and binds his flesh to wood. The world spins, paling only in comparison to the world spinning in their own minds, the twisting and turning of the reality surrounding them.

Sathe never saw his biological mother, Tonne. He never spent a moment in her presence, yet he feels her standing in front of him, scolding him, forgiving him, and then loving him. Genue looks into the eyes of her brother. How could hate obliterate this bond? She releases her hands from Sathe's face.

The zombies approach from the fields. They are drawn to the flame. The moths of disparity and empty souls cling to the last glimmer of youth, life, and breath. The *Singularity* has been depriving their existence of a happy ending. Defeated, Sathe's skin begins to harden. He grabs her hands and can feel the heat pouring from her membranes. The amber air shatters the silence, screaming in agony, as gusts of wind tear at his limbs. Green sap continues to flow from his body, awakening dormant life all around.

Genue reaches to the sun. The gift of life has been taking life, killing human kind slowly, as it grows. She pulls the erupting fire to the Earth and flames take over the atmosphere! In an instance the zombies burn to coal, returning to the ashes. All who walk above the surface are engulfed into the glowing flame of the sky. Their existence is erased from the world. The Singularity is overcome. The sun retracts into its home within the universe, shrinking back to the size that will encourage life once again on the planetary creation, Mother Earth. A garden is born at their feet.

Sathe looks one last time at his sister. She is fire. She is life. Genue watches as her only kin transforms. From his fingers vines reach out into branches. The surface of his skin mutates into bark. Seeds pop from his pores and drift away into the air, creating more trees, brush, and plant-life. Genue feels her body pull toward him. As she floats into him he raises his arms to complete the shape and majesty of the great tree he was destined to become.

In Genue's last moments of awareness she watches as Sathe, the only one of her kind, becomes one with the terrestrial sphere. The orchid is now a tree, blooming flowers and leaves where hair and flesh once grew. Genue falls to her knees and curls into a knot. Weakness, drained of life, at the clutches of death. Her mind is clawing to be free, longing for her body to follow. She is released and plunges into a dream. The only dream reality can create, dancing in the consciousness, becoming one with the collected neurological paradise. She is now freed of her purpose.

She sleeps below the seated tree,
whose branches reach above.
Ino – inside, Genue – the Earth
Together they remain, to rest, heal, and rise again.
Into the Earth anew, for peace and love exude.

-THE DIVINE IS SHATTERED-

Her darkest fear is tossed into view,
Tearing her security to shreds.

It is done.

The fire headed queen sits in her velvet armchair.
Tonne swirls her palms over the corner of the arm, sheering the
soft surface with her touch. She exhales and is returned to calm.
Contentment escapes as she stretches her cat-like frame and
rises to her feet.

> All is good. We are back on track and we will
> make another turn around the sun.

Sudne smiles at Tonne. The Earth is back on its proper orbital
alignment with the Sun. Genue and Sathe barely survived the
blazon fury of the exploded star. They are as two magnets
drawn to each other, but at the same time repelled by equal
force. One could obliterate the other, as they are antagonistic of
the situation. The union would turn them both to stone. The
heart of the machine would be the only inhabitant. Where there
is metal, there is technology. The machine will come back.

Sudne has seen the visions. She fears them and cannot tell Tonne of the devastation to come. She closes her eyes. She sees him looking back at her, the Nano. He will destroy it all. Then the waters will fall. Tonne gasps for air. She falls on her knees. Sudne's thoughts, the mental poison, rotting the wavelengths, altering the vibrations, trickle into the collected consciousness. Tonne knew Sudne was hiding something, but not this.

Sudne! What have I seen?

Sudne is torn from the solarium of her daydream. Tonne stumbles toward her, trying to regain her weakened composure. Reading minds is her curse. Her father gave her the telepathic gift before she was thrown into the universe. She needs her powers to ensure honesty and truth. Once she has released her mind into the outer wavelengths, she is drained of energy, unable to stand. She sits on the floor. Sudne runs to her and falls to the ground by her side.

> I saw your thoughts, Sudne. How long have you known of the vibrations? This will have catastrophic effects on us. Humanity cannot breathe in that much oxygen. What is the effect on them? I know you have seen the end.

Sudne chokes back her tears. If the atmosphere settles and the air begins to stir, all will be suffocated by the very same substance used to sustain life. Tonne gathers herself to stand once more. Sudne helps her back to her seat. She must think on this new insight.

Tonne strokes the soft texture of the chair once more as she decides the fate of all who walk upon the surface of her space ship, Mother Earth. Now that she has retained her spirit form, she remembers all that her soul has experienced. She thinks of the time when she saw the flash of light. She knew it was more than just a flicker of the imagination. She knew she saw the truth that day. She drifts into the daydream and is at once reminded of her true lover's kiss and can feel his aura surround her and tease her with his presence.

Essuel sees her standing there, his past from long ago. Of course she would never know her thoughts she left behind. He studies her in the Earthly form, just beginning her life, a young woman with her future in full bloom.

> I promise I will remember you, Essuel. How could I ever forget your sweet rose petal lips or your soft golden hewed hair.

Essuel closes his eyes and feels her skin with his mirage of fantasy. She does not remember the passion she left behind. He thinks back to the promises they made to each other before she made the cross over dimensions.

> This love we will sacrifice for the love of humankind.

Essuel watches his lady in the flesh. She is no different in this life as she was in the last. Her spirit remains the same. He craves to feel her once again, to see completely, her beauty expressed in the three-dimensional plane. Her scorpion sting, with drips of crimson lava, cascade down her back, and entrance Essuel so that he cannot look away.

Tonne feels his stare burning her shoulder and she turns in his direction. She looks closer as she thought she saw a man. There was a deceiving flicker of energy and light, a flash in the air. Slowly moving through the tables and chairs in the food court, she walks to the light. She looks around. She is all alone. Behind her a poster hangs on the otherwise empty cafeteria wall. Tonne turns again and sees the sign for the first time. She reads the address and feels the deja-vu sting in her mind. She knows of this place already.

BIOLARITY - The Solution to the Future!
Interested participants please inquire on location:
Biolarity Lab #1, 2039 Avenue of OASA

Tonne glances over her shoulder to be certain of her solitude as she pulls the paper from the wall. Hiding it away in her bag, she leaves the scene; curious of the solution the future holds. She will go there and see for herself.

Oh that was close! She almost saw me. I wish to have her back in my arms. Tonne, I have promised to remain always with you, even though you don't know me anymore.

Essuel rests his head on his folded arms as he reflects on his moment in the flesh. He traded his powers to the fallen one. He gave it all just to see her and give her the key. She will be the Biolarity. She is the soul of the Inogenue. His precious Tonne, forever trapped in the cycle of the spirit.

Tonne opens her eyes and she is once again in Sudne's company. Her memory returns and she sees the end is near. All that she fought so hard for will fall again. This time, however, the demon is just a boy, the frightened and gutless one, Annuil. She can feel his villainous intent closing in on her purpose. He has returned to his place in the loop of creation, throwing the present back into the past, recreating the cycle of life.

Tonne looks around her new world. There is a nagging feeling in her stomach that Essuel may be wrong. He took the starseeds and now the cosmos are sick. They are dying. The energy source is causing the decay on Earth. She shakes her head in disbelief and tries to return to her love for Essuel. She speaks to Sudne.

> Annuil must be wrong in this. He must be the enemy. Why else has he told his father of the plans Essuel has done. Sudne, I don't know what to feel anymore. I know it was Essuel that led me to the Biolarity. I just don't know what is going to happen of my Earthly daughter. I am afraid for her. I know that her brother will have the last say. He has the dragon's blood. I can feel there is something not right with him.

> My dear Tonne, of course Essuel is an adversary to the Inogenue. He threatens to steal our only livelihood, the starseeds. Look at your posh surroundings. It is all but an illusion to ease your comfort of captivity. Annuil and I will keep you from ever seeing your Essuel again.

> What did you just say? Who are you?

You naive girl. I am Annuil's mother and I have plucked you from the Earth and here you will live until your final day. Essuel will never find this place.

I thought that was Essuel I met when I first arrived here! You told me he was my love!

Slight of hand my dear. You will never see him again.

Tonne knows she was deceived. She fell for the bluff that took her winning hand. She didn't know at the time that the man who she first encountered in this dimension meant to confuse and conceal her. She followed him blindly into her present trap of misfortune.

Tonne screams out in anguish. She has been captured with no one to ever know where she is. She cries out to Essuel that he may hear her desperation. She cries for her soul to endure the future that lies ahead of her. All she can do is watch the story unfold, numbing her pain into the folds of the void, held captive to the machine.

-THE KING STEPS DOWN-

*At what point does something
different become the same?*

Annuil has returned to Venus, the home of his father and of the Inogenue. The sun has been reduced to the size that will nourish life on Earth. His father's plan to burn her surface has been ended. The placid atmosphere remains shaken by the defeat. The only element unaffected is the black matter.

The heavens dim as the starseeds sit in inactivity. The seeds on the Earth will not be returned to the megacosm. They will remain trapped. Essuel won the solar battle, but still must fight the universal war.

Annuil walks over to his father's bed. This will be the last talk they have together. The great King is dying. He sits on the side of the bed and reaches his fingers to hold his father's once powerful hand, now a fist of bones.

> It has been undone father. Essuel found a way
> to reverse the burn of the sun. I could not stop
> him and I know you are disappointed with me.
> I am a failure to your wishes.

Son, I could never fault you for trying. Essuel is stronger than you and that is why I don't want him to have the throne. His mighty ego will destroy all that he touches. It means more to be unpretentious and rule with a fair hand. His empire will crumble under his grandiose command. You will wait son. You will wait for the moment to take over. When all his people are searching for a change to his treacherous hand, you will step in and complete my mission to rid the Earth of Essuel's tainted experiment.

When will I know? Do I live here on the Venetian paradise with mother or return to the Earth of coal.

Annuil, the machine will reemerge. The planet will not survive the mechanisms as they grow in number beneath the surface. Even your brother cannot foresee what damage the upcoming transformation will cause.

Annuil closes his eyes as his father places an open palm on his forehead. He pulses the air to encourage pressure within the room to build around them. The father delivers the history of the Inogenue into the youth of the future king.

Annuil, I have given you the history. The story. Through my fingertips I have given you the path you must follow to succeed in the battle for our family. You must fight your brother. If he continues to spread his greed across the universe we will all surely die, just as I shall pass now. I have done all I can on this plain of existence. I must cross over. Do not mourn my passing and help your soul if Essuel learns that I am no longer alive. Do I have your word, Annuil? You will carry on my legacy and right our history and return the starseeds to the kingdom of the Inogenue.

Yes father, but wait! I have so many questions
that must be answered. I need direction. I need
a leader. I cannot do this on my own. I chose to
side with you father and now you are leaving
me!

Annuil, do not be afraid of your path. This is
your circumstance and divine decree. This is
what it takes to be king. You must pass the
initiation, my son. Go to my writing table and
bring me the box that says *'Penance'* on the
outside.

Annuil walks across the cold tile floor to his father's desk. The
wood is freshly oiled and he can smell the sweet lemon aroma
radiating from the surface. In the center of the desk sits the
black box. He picks it up and walks back to his father's bedside.

Open it and you will find a book. Within the
pages you will write the story I have placed in
your thoughts just now. I want you to tell the
story so the people will fear Essuel. They must
know that he is a dragon. They must know he
will feed off the energy they create with love.
Inside that box you will also find a velvet bag.
Go ahead and take it out. This is the most
important part.

Annuil reaches into the box once more. With his fingers he can
feel the soft texture of the bag. He lifts it to view, reaches inside,
and pulls out an amulet. The dying king smiles at his son. He is
proud to be handing over the majesty of the Inogenue.

This is the key of our people. Whoever holds it
in their possession is the king and holder of all
the power that comes with the title. You may
put it around your neck now. The Inogenue
made this to be a protection from any force in
the universe that may cause them harm. It has
been hidden across the constellations and I have
protected it all these eons for you to have. Wear
it with pride and you will be a great King.

The amulet is heavy on Annuil's neck. It is the shape of a circle mandala with eight intertwining snakelike figures knotting within one another. It is made of pure gold that glows in the Venetian ozone. He can feel his skin burn under the metal. He notices a latch on the back of the jewelry. He releases the latch and sees the fine powder held within.

> You have found the Starfire, the Elixir of Life. Once a man becomes the king he must ingest the powder. You must drink the metals in order to live a powerful life and rule many, however, not now son. This must be done in your solitude. You must fast for forty days. A true king will survive, however, an imposter will die from the starvation alone. Once you have consumed the elixir, you will feel the dynamism of a great ruler.

Annuil sits back and takes in all he has heard. He is accepting his fate as the one who will put the cosmos back to the way it all must be. Now that the fire is out, the people are rebuilding and repopulating. Time is limited. He looks to his father but is too late to say goodbye. The old king is dead. His father is gone forever to return to the source, the collected consciousness of the neural seed of life.

> My father has passed. I, Annuil, am now the King of the Inogenue. There is to be no word that this has all taken place. If Essuel learns of my title he will demand a war and he will not stop until the blood is liberated from my flesh. He wants my throne!

Annuil looks from his father's deathbed. He feels the weight of responsibility on his shoulders, the tender nudge from the universe in his favor. His thoughts churn within the folds of his prodigy. He reaches down and strokes the surface of his home planet, Venus, the Love Goddess, as she speaks to him through the tips of his fingers.

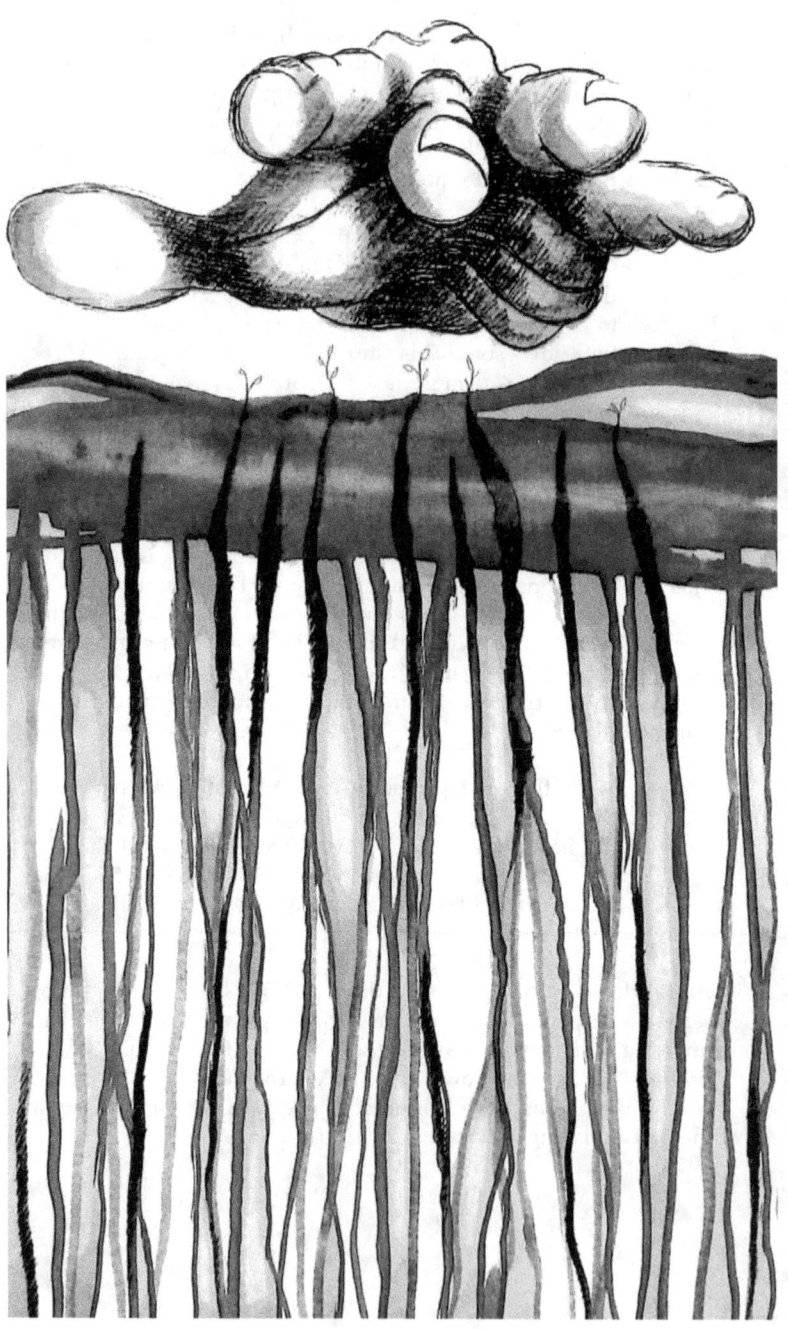

There will be a devastation on the Earth greater than the solar burn of my father. Essuel's mother ship will be drowned within her life sustaining force. All will be drown in her tears.

Annuil smiles as he envisions his brother's torment as all the humanoid creatures choke on the matter that nourishes life. He takes his amulet in his hand and feels the warm metal inside his fist. The Starfire will give him the power to defeat Essuel, the future Dragon King.

+ + + + + + +

The static flickers and the father is led into an imagined death. All who fall are not lost. It is within the soul, the precious starseed, that always knows. The father watches as his sons walk away, turning their back to the choice of love. He has planned this knowing Essuel would betray him. He knew Annuil would in turn betray his own brother to seek his father's love. In weakness, his boys were tempted by the sorcerer's shrew, her face of anger, erasing peace with treason. They ate the fruit of greed and drank from the flask of desire.

The Earth will turn another day. The father will let his terra forma goddess go as he enters the fifth dimension, the miraculous world, and relinquishes the battle between good and evil to those left behind. He leaves his sons a legacy, one that both will fight for domination. Sathe and Genue are the fleshly bond of Essuel and Annuil in spirit, siblings clawing to claim the beauty of the adored Mother Earth. Ahead his maker awaits his arrival. His time of judgment is here.

I feel that I have let you down, my Father.

You have, but I forgive you for that. You are still a child in your own soul evolution.

My boys betrayed me and each other. I failed to teach them the love.

Son, you had to serve your penance for Essuel. You couldn't leave the dragon war alone could you?

I just thought that if there was a union...

Then why didn't you give your life for theirs? The dragon king would have taken in the boy and his mother as an honor upon your sacrifice. You let her down and you led the boy into the trail of darkness.

But father, it was Annuil's life I created with my rightful wife. I promised her my life upon our birth. I could not betray her because of my cursed love for Tia. I made a choice of honor to our society, but I caused a great shame to my bloodline. I am sorry for them both.

You must think of a way to fix what you alone have created. I must send you back, but only on the condition that you show them love.

How can I right this with Essuel without his mother, my dragon queen? He will never forgive me for what I did to her.

Tia is alive. I gave the dragon king a fragment of my power in exchange for her life.

You did that for her?

Son, this is all in the plan. It is up to you now to follow the course and set the balance of love. I must go deeper in the void of the nothingness as I am weakened by the history of this situation. Go now and make your legacy strong. When you go back you will defeat the dragon king and return to me my power. It will be easy to do because he had to marry Tia's sister. She is not as powerful as the eldest. He will not bare a son. Go now boy, for you have two sons to follow you in battle!

At once the solar-plex of his pineal sphere expands and his soul is released into the ethereal family that welcomes him into the collected consciousness of the Inogenue. The father will return to his sons. He will return to the confusion of life to heal the wounds of his family.

-THE LEADER IS BORN-

Hidden within the human heart lies the glitch,
The only cure lies in the sacrifice.

Genue's eyes open. Reality bites the dream as her body awakens. A new existence is all around, like the days long before, of living in harmony with the sun. Her life has been spared. She is alive. Genue rises, naked, her clothes, only a remaining shadow, have fallen to the ground at her feet.

The tree is the ultimate sacrifice of her brother, her Yan, born unto the Earth to live his days of hell, unable to move. Genue strokes her hand across the bark of Sathe's new skin. Energy ripples across his new form. She steps away. It is done. The prophecy, once before only spoken, is now the truth. The sun is back in its place within the balance of time, returned to a size to give life again, not to take and destroy. The air is at once calm. The fog has been cleared.

Humans, the pure and untouched souls forced into the underworld, come out from below to see the Earth's charred exterior. The machines, victims of Nanotechnology, slaves to the Singularity, were on the surface of the Earth when the sun flooded the atmosphere. Fire burned the flesh and disgust of their lives leaving behind only their decayed coal matter. A whole race is gone. The human machine has been eradicated.

Among the people gathering are the offspring of the Nanotechnology, unaffected by the sun. They were not burned in the sun's blaze. The stranded children witnessed their parents burst into flame and return to ash. Now orphans, they retreat together into the underworld left vacant by the humans now returning to the outer realm, reclaiming their life above the surface. The machine, left by the disease of their parents, creep below, hiding in fear that once the truth is realized, they will be destroyed.

Genue knows of their presence. She knows they will sink beneath the land. She understands the pain of an outcast. She looks out into the crowd forming around her with faces of amazement to be outside. A blanket is passed to her from the mass. She looks down the hill at the people, untouched by the machine. They form a circle around her and the tree that will forever contain her brother. Genue drags her hand through her immense blond tresses: unhidden, alive, and awake. She speaks to those below.

> Your world is returned to normal. It will grow and produce food for nourishment and material to make homes for your families. Treat the Earth and each other with kindness. Respect one another. This is your second chance at a harmonious existence.

She speaks to the crowd of dirty people, tanned by the excrement of their existence below. Frightened children hover beneath their mother's feet. Some have never seen outside the confines of the caverns, a new reality for them to digest, a world of nature at their reach.

> Do not follow me nor look for me. I will find you if I am ever needed in the future. Save your families and live in peace with one another and nature. Love is the only way. Community is the answer.

Genue turns away. She must disappear or they will exploit her. The human heart can choose to be evil. She turns away from the people still frozen in awe of what has happened. Stepping back, Genue looks one last time at Sathe.

> Never cut this tree. It will always bring you life.
> The sap will continue to fertilize your ground.
> The life contained within must never be freed or
> you will all surely die. Do not harm this tree
> because it is half of me. Make it your sanctuary.

Genue walks away wrapped in her blanket, her golden hair dancing around her head like flames flickering in the breath of combustion. Before the people realize, she is gone. The universe is in balance, returned to equilibrium, to rebuild and grow...for now.

Most did not live beyond the exploding sun that day. The only people who survived were those forced into underground societies, living in squalor. Over time, they venture back and inhabit the Earth, creating beauty and prosperity.

Leaders are chosen and children are born. Families grow with amazement. It is the awesomeness that she saved them. He saved them. However, in their ignorance and neglectful eye, an army is emerging. The orphans of the machine grow their hate and plan to justify their parent's demise. Eye for an eye, one murder for another, they seek to avenge their parent's death.

The underground awakens as Hades extends his welcoming arms to the children lost for a cause, open to his fuel for chaos and revenge. The Earthly paradise will soon fall.

-THEY ARE AGAINST HER-

They join together in the hunt for her head,
Not knowing she is standing right outside their grasp.

Leerah sits at the table. She is sharp, trained, and focused. Since the emergence back to the surface, she has sought out the one who owes her an eye. Leerah hunts Genue, tracking her scent like a pirate on a hunt for treasure. Staying one step behind, she plans to catch Genue when she falls. Leerah's intentions are to push her into a trap and her revenge will force Genue to spend the rest of her days on Earth, blind on the right.

The waitress brings the check, throws it on the table, and then struts away. No manners or respect these days, selfish, impervious to the irritation this existence has become. Society built itself up quickly. It is almost as if the underground devastation never happened. Homes and communities set root and have grown into cities. Servants to the drug: the altered experience.

Now, the land is generous, but the leaders are not. Upon their emergence to the top, the crop of confused masses has been indentured into a new breed of slavery, disguised, so very well, as the only way to peace. Like the phoenix, humankind is born again, however, still possessing the strand of greed that will devour the land once more.

Ignorance is the ultimate dream. People choose to ignore the rustling below of the orphaned machine, raising each other in their hate. Amid the rubble, a girl desperately claws her way to the top as the leader of this band of derelicts and delinquents. Her name is Meryn.

Chestnut hair, ivory skin, suited with the drive of revenge, Meryn seeks the one who killed her family, the one who burned her mother alive. Now a grown woman, she still has nightmares of holding her mother's charred fingers in her hand. Coming from a family of afford, her parents were able to maintain the Nanotechnology and remain as human as possible. Meryn never saw the hunger for human flesh from her accomplished mother and father. She lived in a spacious home with ample indoor gardens. It is a stark contrast to the underground misery she has been left to maneuver.

Leerah digs through her wallet for cash. She looks to her counterpart across the table, the angry raven-haired friend she has shared so many conversations of hate for Genue.

> Meryn, you got a dollar or something? I can't
> find my change. I may have left it back at home.

Meryn calmly pulls out a twenty and hands it to her ally. Leerah situates herself and holds her hand in the air with her ticket and money. The waitress walks by and snatches the money, distracted by the man at another table and consequently failing to realize how close she could come to her own demise.

> Did she just SNATCH that out of my hand?

Leerah questions her confidante, looking deeply for permission to cause a scene, to scratch the itch she has to fight. Meryn does not bite. There is so much anger in that one, she thinks to herself. Anything will release the spark into ignition.

> Put away your flint. She is not worth the fight.

Meryn gathers her bag and stands from the table. She refuses to encourage Leerah. There will be blood and it will not be from present company.

Well, I'm snatching my change back. I will not
be disrespected! She has no idea who I am and
what I am capable of doing to her. Don't you
agree?

Meryn shakes her head knowing there will be pain. Her friend
cannot be swayed. The waitress saunters back over to the table,
reaching her hand in the direction of the angry one. Without
hesitation Leerah grabs her hand and stares hard into her frozen
eyes.

SNATCH!   DRAG . . . . .WOOSH!!!

In a flash, Leerah rips the bills from her hand. An easy target,
one must always pay attention. The worst damage comes when
the waitress is dragged across the table and hurled into the wall.
Meryn glares at her associate. The waitress stumbles across the
floor and retreats behind the counter. The other customers have
fled into the street unsure of what just happened.

What? She wouldn't let go. I just led her in that
direction.

And now it is time for us to go.

Leerah smiles at her own strength. Just living in such a close
proximity to Genue all those years seeped sensational strength
into her own presence. She even sometimes drank water after
Genue when they lived together in the underground as
children. It was all trashed when Genue lied to her and took her
eye. She will replace her own empty socket with the crystal blue
sphere of her nemesis. Revenge is near. She can feel her prey
drift into the false security of peace and protection.

Meryn and Leerah exit the restaurant to begin the hunt for the
elusive one. Meryn's angle in joining Leerah's mission is to
reclaim the land that was once hers, a land that was stripped
from her fingertips by Genue. Her hate equals that of Leerah's
hate for stealing her eye. They walk in tandem, planning the
ultimate demise of her innocence. She must be given her
penance.

So the hunt begins. On each side passion ignites.

The prince sits on his throne in the wilderness and absorbs the scene laid out in front of him. Trees of silken emerald color watch him sit in his silence. Blades of sap-filled grass sway in the dance of air, moving slowly to the beat of love emerging, growing, and living. All is right and it is good. So it seems.

It has been written!

He speaks into the air around him as he holds the book close to his chest. It is the journal, a chronicle of days to come. He was sent by the Inogenue to write the story for the people on Earth. The time is before the sun invites itself onto the planet, one last chance to turn the history around. He knows what the story will tell, a prophecy that his father will be angered and will send for the destruction of inhabitants of the luscious planet.

Green bushes and trees grow out of the fertilized ground. Crisp air blows through the silent trees, whispering secrets into the leaves. No one pays attention to the subtle warnings of the vegetation. No one knows the destruction to come. Not yet that is. All will be revealed in the coming time.

He touches to the necklace tied around his neck. The cold metal represents his frigid heart. There is no compassion for the innocent of the land. He rubs his thumb across the filigree surface thinking of the alchemist's dream contained inside, the gift of immortality that lies within. The trees beg him to change the story. They know death is near. The air will turn to fire and the water will boil. *'Please rewrite the tale'*, they plead with him. He shakes his head in defiance. The trees and all life will be burned at the stake. *Penance* will be served to all!

Lowering himself to the warm soil beneath his feet, he lays the book in its final place. It is to be left there on the ground to be discovered by her. It has a purposeful reader. She walks down this same wooded path to her home each day. She will find the book and read the prophecy that lies within.

He looks to the sky. It sings the joy of a perfect day. Clouds roll by as the sun flickers light on his pasty flesh, turning his gaze back to the ground. The girl will keep the story in her heart. She will not believe the contents at first. She will share the story with no one until the time of revelation has come. She will know this in her heart. It is her purpose.

Now await the next chapter.

They say this in whispers to his electrical currents of the mind, a soft breeze of air speaking into his ear. He stands from the ground and walks back to civilization, leaving his testimony behind to await her discovery. He will share these words of peace and redemption, fear and deception, a betrayal to make the space for love and hate.

> *Share this book with all those who posses an open mind to listen and an open heart to care. The prophecy has been delivered. Now stand back and watch your fate or have the collective courage to change the path of darkness.*

He clinches his fists tightly. They are sore from his burden, the mission he must see until completion, the only reason for his life. Chaos is his only outlet, the accomplice to his secret. He will lead the war that will encourage the destruction of his father's lovely planet. Jealousy rages in his chest as he leaves the scene, his black coat slaps his ankles and dances to the rhythm of his steps.

The tale of the cosmos, the story of the alternate truth, is left behind. He dreams of the future, all of which he has seen before in the collected consciousness. He has seen the technology and the malfunctioned humans. He has seen the underground and the pained faces that plead for another day. Laughter escapes as he daydreams of the evil this revelation will unearth. The fear his story will encourage brings pleasure to his tortured mind. A malicious smile overcomes his lips as he licks his teeth, a habit he has come to rather enjoy.

HE WILL HAVE HIS DAY TO LOOK THE DRAGON IN
THE EYES AND BREATHE FIRE INTO THE DARKNESS,
BURNING IN THE ASHES THAT WILL CONSUME
WHAT WAS ONCE THE MIGHTY LIGHT.

www.ingramcontent.com/pod-product-compliance
Lightning Source LLC
Chambersburg PA
CBHW071235130626
46556CB00003B/1025